Eliana Marrocchella

Lessons Learned

Majoring in Life Series,
Book Two

Copyright

ISBN 978-0-9600077-1-4

TABLE OF CONTENTS

Copyright Page

Dedication

Forward

Acknowledgment

Quote

DEDICATION

To my amazing first-generation Italian-American parents who taught my siblings and me to love the arts and to combine artistic creativity with the logical side of life. Life without good parents is so difficult. I can't imagine what my life would have been like without my parents' love, guidance, and support.

They always put our wants and needs ahead of theirs, holding us up above the drowning currents of life's hardships. They not only taught us how to live, but they also *demonstrated* how to live—every day of their lives.

They taught us to put God first, family next, and then the individual. They demonstrated how to be more than a Sunday Christian. They showed us how to love even when it is an impossible task. They asked us to always do our best. And most important, to forgive. Thank you, Mom and Dad, for giving us such a great start.

Contact Information:

https://www.amazon.com/~/e/B07XF67PRX

https://www.facebook.com/e.marrocchella

emarrocchella@hotmail.com

www.emarrocchella.com

https://twitter.com/LovesTeaching11

FORWARD

Eliana Marrocchella (Marrow-KEL-la) knew when she was little that she wanted to be an English teacher. In the middle of her first year of teaching, she made an observation that I'll never forget. She told me, "You know that I haven't used much of the knowledge I learned in college, but I have used what I've learned in life's classroom."

She continued, "Life constantly teaches you, so much so that you ought to be able to major in it. You will never complete life's teachings, though, until the day you die." She also said she threw away most of what she learned in college and relied on life's lessons when it came to teaching.

Eliana is the best for writing this book because for years, before she taught the great love stories, she taught the concepts of limerence—scientifically and humorously known as an affection deficiency disorder (otherwise known as love at first sight or romantic love). She based this whole series on the psychological concept of limerence!

What I liked most of all about this book is that I think the college atmosphere that she suffers through each day is like one of the major characters of the book. It's this old relative/friend she keeps going back to because she has to deal with it. One that forces her to interact with other people from all walks of life where she has to experience different beliefs and morals. Yes, it gives her a chance at independence, but it also tempts her everyday with vices like alcohol, drugs, handsome men, and the freedom to make choices. Good or bad choices.

I enjoyed learning—or relearning—life's lessons right along with Domenica and Matt. Now the question is: Can we learn all about love and then apply it?

 Enjoy the love story,
Kacie Cox

ACKNOWLEDGMENTS

I would like to acknowledge my best friend Karen, of "many" years, who gave me words of encouragement to just go for it. I would also like to acknowledge Saya from Red Quill Editing who was never too busy for any question I had and who commended the good parts of my book, but also *nicely* told me when I was sputtering like an old Model-T Ford. Lastly, my children and many years of high school students who loved me as much as I loved them. They taught me many things, but the three most important are:

 - If you look for the good in a person, you will certainly find it.
 - Children can learn anything if you teach the way they learn and allow them to learn at their own pace.
 - If you give love freely, you get it back in abundance.

~

Cover photo of "G Anthony" courtesy of *Mary Beth Holland Photography.* Thanks Mary Beth for kindly helping a new author.

Model: **G. Anthony** —Thanks G, my *son* from another *one*!

Cover photo of "Sidney Sebold Poolside Photo" courtesy of Tommy Mac Fotos. Thanks Tommy for kindly helping a new author.

Model: Sidney Sebold — "Sidney Sebold Poolside Photo." Thanks Sidney. Your beauty on the outside matches your beauty on the inside.

Edited by
Red Quill Editing
Your Story Told Your Way

Sometimes,

temptation comes disguised

in sky blue eyes

that can tantalize.

~ E. Marrocchella ~

Chapter 1

"Remember a few months ago I told you about a possible problem that you might have to take care of for me?" Taking a drag on his cigarette, Colonel James Masters leaned back in his creaking leather office chair, his shirt stretched over hidden fat that rolled over his belt. "So can you do it or not? The price is still five hundred thousand." He was not afraid to speak on his secured phone line as he pressed the phone between his shoulder and ear allowing him to sign a few more forms on his desk.

"Holy shit! It must be a large problem to offer me that much to get rid of it." Slouched back comfortably in the deep pillows of his couch, Kade Abraham glanced at the muted baseball game on TV while he conversed with Masters.

"Just a fucking mongrel that thinks it's a fucking champion purebred. It needs euthanized. A goddamn threat to this organization and our country. I want this done quickly, so I've given you an incentive to do just that."

"Who is it?"

"A Matt Hoover."

A chill went through Kade's body even as his eyes bugged out from shock. He stiffly sat up. *What the fuck did Matt do now? How could he be an enemy of the United States?*

"I'll send you the specifics as to where he might be now. It should be an easy job for you once you find him."

"As soon as I see the money in my off-shore account, consider it done." He still couldn't believe it. Matt had betrayed his country.

"Oh, and one other thing. There is a woman involved."

"Isn't there always?" Kade sneered into the phone figuring that this was why Matt had strayed. The woman they'd talked about. How she had her clutches dug into him.

"He's not with her now, but he may try to communicate with her. I'd start with her. Use the same identity we've established for the past five years. The rich real estate investor."

"That's feasible."

"You've really come out ahead with that profile we created for you. How many real estate offices do you have now?"

"Four." He knew the Colonel was subtly pointing out how Kade had made a killing in the real estate business. "When I asked, you *did say* I could develop that persona to make it look believable. Who knew I would be so good at commercial real estate? I actually make inconceivable amounts of money!"

"Thanks to me sending you connections too. Just remember that. Oh! And I'm warning you about the girl. She is intelligent, beautiful, and built like a brick shithouse. I'm paying you extra not to entrap yourself in her enticing web. By that, I mean her pussy. That bitch could almost sway me, maybe even Jesus Christ Himself!"

"You don't have to worry. You know I'm the fuck-'em-and-leave-'em kind of guy."

"I'm counting on it." The Colonel took another long drag and blew out the smoke. His chair creaked as he leaned up to his desk. "You know how this works. I deposit half now and half when you finish the job. I'll make the deposit in the morning."

Click.

"Just what I like. A man who is tight on words and loose with money." Kade placed his cell phone on the side table and glanced out the window.

What he hadn't planned on was a contract on someone he considered a friend—Matt. Good ol' Lima Bean. Matt had probably sided with the wrong people—maybe the girl involved—for the right amount of money. The right temptation can quickly change a man's moral views. It's funny how life plows through and changes things you never even thought possible.

At that moment, his mind plunked him back into his Apache helicopter in the middle of one of his many battles during his military deployments.

Through his helmet, Kade heard the chatter from all the pilots of the engaged Apaches. They had to open a twenty-mile pathway so the enemy could not assault the ground convoys on their way to Kuwait. Still not quite dawn, all he could see was the black and green silhouettes moving like floating ghosts through his night vision.

Lawrence Lucas Cooley, nicknamed LL, honed in on a target. The other pilots labeled him with that nickname because he listened to all rap music; he just loved LL

Cool J even though, when he rapped along with the lyrics, his words were usually way off from all of the originals.

Orville Watson, known as Orville, the Hillbilly, was in formation in his bird next to Killer Kade zooming in on a target. The pops of the 30mm and the whoosh of the rockets made it difficult to hear their chatter.

"One-Three, this is One-Five." Orville called out.

"Go ahead One-Five." Kade responded.

"Roger. Target Destroyed. Send us another one."

"Roger, One-Three. Call tally on targets left of my spot."

"One-Five. Tally Targets."

"Get over there quick! Quick! I see another target." Kade countered as he had a visual of enemy movement on the ground.

Swoosh! Boom!

"Heeeee-haw! We got it!" Orville's voice screeched over the communications system again. With Orville's trademark call and name, Kade had to laugh thinking how the other pilots teased him about being a Tennessee hillbilly.

"Okay. Great hit! Good job, Hillbilly. No targets found over here," Kade responded as he perused his area.

LL jumped in, "Roger that. We are about three kilometers left of you. Hey, I'm night stalkin' our enemy; I'm a flying fuckin' killin' choppa'." LL always threw in Cool J's lyrics—or what he thought were the lyrics—into his comms. Of course, they weren't even close! He messed up the words every single time.

Suddenly, Kade noticed movement on the ground. "All players be advised. One on the move running eastbound. Wait! …Okay, they shot him… That mover now sitting. He's stationary."

"Roger. He's wounded. No weapons seen." Orville responded to Kade.

"Oh. Damn!" Kade watched as the mover sitting on the ground jumped up to run again. Suddenly, his body jerked from an apparent bullet and fell limp. "Okay… He's dead now."

LL came back in. "Wait! I got four individuals over here! We will be engaging. You are afraid cuz I'm a self-made pilot fucker, and you know I'll invade you and blow your asses up to fuckin' pieces.'" A few chuckles were heard over the comms because once again his lyrics weren't even close this time.

At that second, Kade screamed out a warning to the others. "Shots fired just below our position! Shots fired!"

Orville screamed back. "RPG taking fire! Taking fire! Everybody engage. Engage!"

"Orville, come on, come on! Move!" Kade knew Orville was in some deep shit right now.

"One-Three coming hard left!" Orville warned the others.

LL jumped into the conversation. "Be advised we just blasted that guy shooting. He is no longer with us. Repeat. No longer a threat. LL always got you guys covered. 'We gonna win this battle, we gonna make you feel a whole lot of rattle shit. Cuz I'm an Army soldier.'"

Kade noticed two vehicles up ahead, so he reported to the ground force commander at the Tactical Operations Center (TOC), "Sir, we have two vehicles northbound, a truck with individuals in the back and a van. Is this your HVT sir?"

"Roger. Continue to let us know where they are going."

"Roger. They are entering the eastern grid." Kade maneuver the Apache to follow them.

"Roger. If you are PID of weapons, you are clear to engage. I repeat clear to engage."

Silent John Cattoi was the gunner in front of Kade and abruptly screamed out, "I see weapons. Repeat! Weapons on board!"

"Engage! Engage!" Kade put his finger on the trigger and squeezed. A few seconds later Boom! Boom! Both vehicles exploded into puffs of fire and a white plume of smoke.

The Apaches made one more sweep of the area with LL calling into the TOC. "Targets all eliminated, request to return to base. "Ain't no Marine can hang wid us…Thung ass Army aviators that love to blow up shit.'" His reference to Notorious B. I. G's "Notorious Thugs" was so off that this time hysterical laughter sounded through the comms system!

Someone now called out over the comms. *"Hey LL! Have you <u>ever</u> actually heard any of these songs?"* This brought more quieted chuckles.

"Roger that," the ground commander answered. *"And a warning to keep your raps under wrap especially since your words are so bad no one can even recognize the song! You sound like the white ass cracker that you are! Ain't no timin' in yo' rhymin.' Zero-Six out."*

"Yesssss sirrrrr!" LL responded with everyone bursting out laughing at the commander's response, but more so at LL's terrible ability to rap. The pilots all realized that, based on the ground commander's non-disciplinary response, he appreciated what they'd accomplished today.

The radios were silent. The sun was now rising over the horizon, a beautiful view from in the sky. The pilots still were not sure if it was safe below. Although Kade always knew to maintain a porcupine appearance, he couldn't wait to get back to base to relax.

Suddenly cutting into their silence, they all heard it. *"TIC, TIC, TIC! This is Hard Road Zero-Eight on guard."*

The hair on Kade's neck stood up. He immediately knew. Troops In Contact. Before he could key the mic, he heard a response from another aircraft on the radio.

"Hard Road Zero-Eight. Thunder Seven-One is a flight of two F-16's. What do you need?"

"Identify yourselves," the ground commander piped in.

"This is Hard Road Zero-Eight. We need suppression and extraction! We're under fire. Returning from a mission. One man injured."

Zero-Six responded, *"What's the letter of the day, Zero-Eight?"* Kade listened in as the commander asked for the letter of the day to verify they were Americans and not a trap to lure the military in for a rescue. There was always an official letter of the day that all military knew for verification.

"Zero-Six, this is Zero-Eight. Don't know. We went out a few days ago and been out without contact. Our mission went bad. We have one injured… and are taking fire."

"We need the letter of the day."

"What the fuck don't you understand about we've been out a few days?" The desperate voice screamed into the radio.

"No letter, no support," came the somber reply.

Kade came into the conversation. *"Hard Road Zero-Eight, what's your position?"*

"We are three kilometers east of Objective Python on foot."

"Roger. We're about two minutes out."

"I'll back you up," LL called out.

The commander tapped in after LL. *"What didn't you guys understands? No letter, no pick up!"*

Kade came in again. *"What's that, Zero-Six? You're break…up… in… Sir? I bl…Tow…ka… Sir?"*

"Your fucking ass is mine when you get back, One-Four!" the commander screamed back at him.

"Zero-Six! This is One-Four," Kade responded with a devious smile spreading on his face. *"Come in over… Damn. We lost comms with the TOC. Let's go get those guys and get back home, LL. I think the TOC had something important to tell us!"* Kade, although smiling, knew the commander wanted to kill him right now.

"Okay. That's a roger. Damn, the reception is bad here," LL threw into the conversation accentuating the bad reception in an attempt to cover Kade's ass.

Kade turned to the coordinates thinking how dumb the TOC was. All Kade had to do was fly over low and see if the guys below were Americans. How the fuck hard was that? In no time, he and LL were in the vicinity.

"I have PID of friendlies, one o'clock about 3k."

"Tally, I got them," LL responded.

"Hard Road Zero-Eight, from your position where's enemy force?"

"Zero-Eight has maybe two trucks, five to ten dismounts to our northwest about three hundred meters."

"One-Four Tally targets. In bound hot! LL, cover us. Shoot anything that isn't friendly and moves." Kade directed.

"Already on it." It took about ten seconds with a few momentous booms for the radios to squeal with LL's voice, "Zero-Eight, threat eliminated."

Kade returned to the men on the ground. "Zero-Eight, move about seventy-five meters east of your position to the open area. First, for verification that you're American military, I want to know who the American actress is with the biggest tits."

Five laughing voices instantly screamed out in unison.

"Pamela Anderson!"

"Charlotte McKinney!"

"Jennifer Love Hewitt"

"No! Beyonce!"

"Okay, okay! That's verification enough for me." Kade heard LL's boisterous laughter. "I'm on my way down. When I get there, you better already be up in the air hopping onto the air craft wings."

"Roger that. Thanks for the pickup."

Maneuvering his aircraft down to the field, Kade planted it in the center of the open area. The small group of friendlies ran out from the brush, one behind and one in the front, while two in the middle carried a third.

Suddenly shots pierced the air. Ping! Ping! They plunged to the ground as Kade lifted off.

"LL, fix that fucking problem quick!" Kade yelled out.

"I'm on it." Pops from the 30mm sang out kicking up the brush, dirt, and even a few dead bodies. Then all was quiet, except for the rumbles of the choppers.

"Problem solved, One-Four."

Kade came down into position. The men raced to the chopper securing themselves to the wings and making sure their injured comrade was safely bound to the craft.

"Okay?" Silent John gave a thumbs up. When he saw the returned gesture, he added, "Let's go home, guys. Beer's on you tonight."

Kade lifted his helicopter into the sky and headed back to the base. The distinct stereo sounds of whoop-whoop, whoop-whoop, whoop-whoop rang out around the two helicopters until they finally reached the base with their precious cargo onboard. After they landed and the engines rattled to stillness, the men all met at the side of the aircraft as medics carried Darrell to CASH, the military support hospital.

"Thanks, guys," Matt yelled over to Kade and LL. "Thanks. Man, you just saved five lives.

"Hey, never leave a soldier behind, right?" Kade extended his right hand and Sergeant Matt Hoover grasped it with a firm handshake. "I'm Kade "Killer" Abraham and this is Silent John Cattoi. This here is LL Cooley and his co-pilot, that's John "Hard Rider" Stevens."

"I'm Matt Hoover. That's Darrell Phillips on his way to CASH. This here's Jimmy Bellino, Mike Cannon, and Peewee Adamson." They all shook hands at their introductions.

Matt put his left hand on Kade's shoulder and squeezed it as he repeated, "I really mean thank you, man. You didn't have to pick us up. I'll talk to my Captain so you don't get into trouble. Just thanks again."

"By the way, the letter of the day is L-Lima." Kade knew the enemy would have killed Matt and the others if he had obeyed his commander. What's worse is that they knew it, and

the TOC knew it. He hoped he and LL weren't in a lot of trouble. Trouble or no, he couldn't let American soldiers die when he had a feasible chance of saving them.

***

"I don't give a fuck if you couldn't hear me on the intercom. No letter, no pick up! Do you understand, Chief?" All the pilots that had gone on the combat mission were in the company TOC listening to a debriefing of their mission from the commander.

Kade stood up. "I. Will. Never. Leave. An. American soldier. Behind. Ever!" With that statement, he stood and walked out of the debriefing knowing that he would be insubordinate. The commander could do with him whatever he wanted.

"Chief!" He shouted louder. "Chief! I suggest you get your ass back to your seat!" The commander was almost screaming now. Kade kept walking because he knew if he returned, he would head right for the ground commander and beat the shit out of him.

"I won't leave an American soldier either." Following Kade's example, LL stood and moved to the aisle.

"Me neither," responded Silent John standing up and then walking out.

"Nor me." LL's co-pilot, Hard Rider, followed Silent John.

All of a sudden, all the pilots on the mission stood and walked out to the amazement of the officers standing up front. "Get back here now!" The command's voice fell on deaf ears.

From wondering how he would fare in jail to his chest now swelling up with pride, Kade allowed a sly smile to pass over his face as he made his way to his chu, his own private area to relax and maybe get some sleep. He knew no commander in his right mind would want to explain to the upper echelon why all the pilots had walked out on him. For now, as he returned to his quarters, he was safe.

He was just about to throw himself on his bed when Silent John came into his room. "Hey, there are some guys here to see you." Behind him stood Matt Hoover and two of Matt's men, Peewee Adamson and Mike Cannon. Silent John continued, "Alright if I help myself to some apple juice?"

"Yeah, go ahead." Kade responded.

As Silent John poured himself some apple juice, Matt extended his hand to Kade.

"Hey, Lima Bean! How many times you gonna thank me?" Kade grabbed his hand as the other two men followed behind Matt with hands extended.

"Maybe for the rest of our lives, since you're the reason we have lives."

Another pilot came into Kade's room, "Kade, I'm just gonna help myself to some apple juice. I won't interrupt." Kade nodded to him.

Kade, truly humbled by the reaction of Matt and his men, shook all their hands and replied, "I would think there would be many guys in the military that would have done the same thing I did. No big deal. But you could pay me back by introducing me to one of your sisters."

"No fucking way!" Mike yelled. "We heard how you are with the ladies."

Laughter filled the air as another pilot walked in on their conversation. He pointed to the bottle of apple juice, then to his glass. Kade waved him on. The pilot helped himself and quietly walked out of the room, as Kade asked, "By the way, how's Darrell?"

"Gonna live because of you. Listen, Kade. We'd like to invite you over to our compound for some beer just to thank you physically."

Two more pilots walked in going straight for the apple juice.

"What the fuck is it with these pilots and apple juice? Is it something good for flying?" Matt definitely looked confused.

Kade's threw his head back as his heavy laughter filled the room. He walked over to one of the apple juice bottles and poured some of the clear golden topaz-colored liquid into a few

glasses. He handed the glasses to Matt, Peewee, and Mike saying, "Whatever you do, don't
drink this apple juice down too fast."

Matt smelled, then tasted the apple juice, and a slow smile smeared across his face.
"Whiskey in an apple juice bottle?"

"Just a little Gentleman Jack for unit morale." The words rolled off his tongue, as did
the whiskey, with an air of connoisseurship. "A friend in the States sends it to me in a few
apple juice bottles every month, since it is illegal to send whiskey. I drink it for the 'vitamin
C.'" Kade formed quotation marks in the air as he said apple juice and vitamin C.

Into the night, they finished a bottle and a half of Gentleman Jack as they talked about
missions they went on, women they fucked, and what assholes some commanders were. For
the next few weeks, Matt and Kade continued to spend a lot of time together in their spare
time, enjoying the camaraderie that only soldiers share. By the end of their tours, they had
become good friends.

Kade drifted out of his reverie and asked the definitive question aloud,
"What the fuck did you do, Lima Bean?" He started to remember how he told
Matt about the job with the other government agency, called an OGA. It was
an agency not directly affiliated with the military or our government. It did
what the government or military couldn't do legally. Kade also told him not to
mention his name when Matt interviewed for the job. Kade didn't even worry
about Matt getting a position, because with Matt's military record, his shooting
ability as a sniper alone would make him the number one recruitment
candidate.

The Colonel still had no clue the two knew each other. In the business they
were in, it wasn't as if they would be invited to barbeques at the Colonel's
home. Pretty much, no one knew anyone else.

Kade would find out what treasonous thing Matt was involved in and, if it were serious enough, he *would* kill him without a second thought. America had no room for traitors. Hell, if the woman was involved, he would kill her too—as a freebie.

Chapter 2

You wake up and follow your life's patterns just to plow through the monotonously long seconds of the days. Maybe use the bathroom first, maybe make coffee first—the same morning routine before leaving for work only to return home, eat supper, watch TV, go to bed, and start that same process all over again tomorrow.

Without love, life becomes this uninterrupted, mediocre plodding through the timeline of human life—what Matt's life had become without Domenica. No bumps, no curves. Like a song with one word, one note, and one chord. Flat. Dull.

Yes, Matt Hoover was now living a lifeless life without his soul mate. Little did he know on that late afternoon in Atlanta, when he first saw her at the bar she was tending, that he would truly become alive in an instant, only to eventually succumb once again to a kind of death. His body was back to trudging through the monotonous patterns of mere existence.

For that one brief moment, his life's timeline had merged with the Domenica Bartholomew timeline. That one major point of all the events in his life—when he first saw her. Before that point, his timeline was colorless and bland.

That same point during their shared lives marked the days with Domenica as vibrantly kaleidoscopic. To him, this monumental event changed everything forever. In the vast sense of things, he realized two unknown people sharing their moment in time would never make it into the history books of humanity's greatest events. Let's face it. On the hierarchy of all human life, they were the two lowly, unimportant beings on the bottom of the pecking order.

Then there was the other major point on his timeline. The day he had to leave her. Where his timeline separated from hers, where he went back to living the mottled shades of black, white, and gray.

"You got those pots done yet?" The short-order cook Billy asked.

"Just a few more. Do you need one of them now?"

"The smaller pot."

Matt hurried and cleaned it for him.

He stood over the old Hobart dishwasher in the back of the small diner, rinsing off the greasiest dirty dishes before he sent them into the mouth of the roaring metal machine. He washed the big silver pot in the duel sink, rinsed it, and stacked it on the side to dry. Those steel giants were piling up because of lunch hour. He eventually would catch up and then be done for the day to return to his small room at the boarding house.

For the last three months, Matt continually worked odd jobs for cash so he could stay off the grid. He probably had the best operatives, who worked for his prior employer, trying to find him to kill him. Yes, cash was the way to go. He knew how they thought, how they planned, how they would act, because he used to be one of them. Men hired to legally kill America's untouchable criminals.

After he left the army, he was recruited, actually enticed, into an OGA to help save America by killing America's enemies. What a bunch of bullshit propaganda he fell for. Except this OGA, the one that suckered him into it, was responsible for not only unethical actions, but illegal ones as well.

Matt tried to quit, especially after the Colonel contracted him to kill a woman—not that he had a problem killing a woman. In this case, however, her child was with her as she was coming out of a mall. He aimed and gently pulled the trigger. She fell to the ground as the little boy watched. Just like that, it was a matter of a few seconds to complete the job.

The problem for Matt was that he later found out from Colonel Masters himself that her death was to draw her husband to the states so the USA could arrest him as a drug lord. She was an innocent. She had never done anything wrong—except fall in love with the wrong man. That was the eye-opening incident for Matt. Kill an innocent to capture a criminal. The guilt that she might not have been the only innocent he'd killed was crushing him.

Matt could not live with that anymore. As a result, when he threatened to expose their actions, he became a threat to the OGA's man in charge, Colonel James Masters. So now, Masters wanted him dead. He actually had plotted for Matt to die at the hands of the Secret Service on his last assignments. Even though they shot him, he survived.

If not for Domenica's friends helping him to heal and sneak away, he most certainly would have died. He had to flee from the organization to protect himself and the ones he now loved.

He now lived off the grid. He moved from city to city working various odd jobs in small mom and pop diners, all the while making his way to

Washington, DC. There he would find the pompous Colonel James Masters, the man who had put out a contract on him, the man he would enjoy killing.

There was only one way to stop the mess he was in, and that was to do what he did best, kill the few people who knew about his work at the OGA, the ones who were after him. He also had to attempt what would probably end up being a suicide mission: to enter their secured building and eliminate his file from Colonel Masters' office computer.

The good thing about his job was that since the OGA performed everything in secrecy, they only kept assassins' profiles on a few computers, so if any government investigation *should* arise, only one or two computers would have to be destroyed. The computer he needed would be in the Colonel's office.

Perhaps then, he could make his way back to Domenica Bartholomew, the young woman who had awakened his soul by showing him a world of living color, who made him understand what being human meant. She inadvertently made him realize that the worst thing in life a person could do was to live life without a reason to live life, to exist simply because one was born.

She changed all that for him. Even if he had to be this dying star, his imploding into a black hole would suck in his enemies also so that nothing remained but a void. If he died in that building, at least Domenica and those who loved her would never have to worry again. They would be safe.

"Mark? You got those dishes done?" Smitty Baker, the owner of the diner, called Matt by his false identity. Matt had access to five different identities all of which included a birth certificate, driver's license, a military record, a resume built from bogus jobs, and a passport. The problem was he could only use them at these small jobs, because if he tried to leave the country or open a bank account or credit card, his predators would be watching and would find him. At this job, he was Mark Stiner.

With his special ops background, he knew how to survive. When the OGA provided the fake ID's, he became best friends with the man who created them. Repaying a personal favor to Matt, Bruce Watkins made him a few more identities under the table so to speak, just in case he needed to disappear from everyone. Mark Stiner was under the table, off the grid, an unperson in an unlife.

Mark Stiner was a vet suffering from PTSD. He was homeless. He could not maintain a good job, so he asked for cash because he did not have a bank account. He had to pay for his room at various cities with the cash he earned. Yes, everybody bought the story and tried to help the veteran-in-need. It didn't hurt that by paying him cash, employers did not have to have any paper work on him that would make them have to pay more into social security or workers' comp. It was a win/win situation for everyone.

"Yeah, Smitty," he replied. "I'll be done in an hour if you want to give me my cash for the week."

"Got it right here." Smitty handed him his weekly envelope.

Matt finished the dishes, wiped down the stainless steel prep tables, waved a hearty good-bye to the other workers, and left to return to his room where he continued to plan his strategy on erasing himself from his former job. Matt slid into 'Mark Stiner's' old clunker and drove to the boarding house.

Hopefully, Mrs. Collier, the kind owner, would have some dinner saved for him. She always put aside food for him because he never knew if he was going to have to work overtime at the restaurant. As the door slammed behind him, he saw her bustling to him with that beaming smile on her face as she wiped her hands on her gingham apron. She was a roly-poly woman, gray hair with a hanging bosom where she probably rocked her grandchildren to sleep. The aroma of dinner wafted under his nose like a kitten's lithe body rubbing against him.

"I saved you some chicken pot pie. A nice big piece, with a couple of homemade biscuits. I thought you also might like a salad."

"Thanks, Mrs. Collier. I know I say it all the time, but I really do appreciate you preparing a dish for me every night I'm late." He gave her a bear hug, took his care-package plate, and went up the steps to his room to do some research on his laptop.

He hacked the Washington, D.C. Building Inspections Department and retrieved a copy of the blueprints of the building where the OGA was housed. How ironic, using the very information the OGA taught him against them. From this print, he would figure the fastest way in and, most importantly, out of the building. He needed to study elevators, stairs, rooftops, vents, everything that could get him in and out unnoticed. It would be another long night.

Chapter 3

This class was terrible! Domenica's professor was as boring as hell and incapable of change, maybe because he came in at biblical Abraham's age of one hundred seventy-five! He actually docked her two points for writing *he/she* instead of *he* on her final essay. After class, she went up to his desk to question this by reminding him that *he/she* or *he or she* was grammatically correct. His answer? "Not in my class."

She could have fought it, but she had an A going and did not want to rock the boat so to speak. However, if her grade became a B, there would be repercussions for this professor. She had kept a notebook on what he said, did, and taught. This little ploy actually saved her in quite a few of her classes. Her various professors had to change three grades to what they should have been when she went to the deans of the particular departments with complaints of their teaching methods, their behavior, or proof of her actual grade.

Right now, though, this current old fucker with his own grammar rules! This would be one of the things she would not miss when her college days were over. The fact that professors had their own way of writing, with students having to change to accommodate each professor, whether it was grammatically correct or not.

Anyway, it was soon time to go. The torture of this class was over, and by the end of the week, all of her spring finals would be done. Now, she could go to the natatorium for diving practice to unwind and let the water wash away her endlessly empty days.

She thought about Matt—always. She wondered if he was safe. She did not know if she would ever be able to forget him, her first real love, the one she was looking for, her soul mate. He was the one she gave herself to for the first time. She was happy with him, complete with him.

Then their whirlwind nightmare occurred. Someone shot at them, someone chased them, and someone bugged her apartment with Matt explaining that he was a hired sniper, a nice term for an assassin for a governmental OGA. This organization *could* do and they *did* do anything they wanted. They actually did end up trying to kill him. But with her good friends, Jamal Jackson and Dawan Owens, she had helped him hide until he healed. Then they'd helped him to escape.

She had not seen him since, nor heard from him. It had been over three months and spring quarter was almost at an end. Life is so long when you can feel every second of every day.

Her mental pain wore upon her soul. When she had a sore muscle from a workout, she only had to stretch out to alleviate the pain for a while. There was no workout for emotional pain. A person had to endure and hope time would assuage the agony of it.

Her physical pain was a hole in her heart that just would not close. She chocked up another lesson learned. She once told Matt that college was more about learning life's lessons than learning knowledge. She learned a lot about herself with this first true experience of loving someone unconditionally: Love was not for anyone weak of mind or soul. A person had to be strong and have plenty of courage to handle the pain and suffering it carried along with it. A lesson she almost failed when he left her.

As she headed into the locker room, she glanced at her reflection in the mirror. She used to have a brightness to her skin. Now, with stress and sadness a constant in her life, she realized she should apply some concealer to the dark circles under her eyes. Oh well, diving into the water would just wash it away anyway. Too bad no makeup company ever manufactured a type of concealer to hide the scars that developed on a person's heart after it had been ripped up and slowly pieced back together. Heart scars were the ugliest.

She changed into her suit and headed toward the board climbing up swiftly to start practicing her dives. Coach Jeffries was still upset with her, because right after Matt left, she had her championship meets. At that time, she really was not in the right frame of mind to dive or do much of anything for that matter. This cost the team dearly. Domenica could not even tell him why she was not there mentally.

Hey, Coach! I just found out the love of my life kills people. Now he's gone into hiding so he won't be killed. Oh yes, I could be killed too, or my family and friends, but I will forget all of that and dive the perfect dive just for you! Go Team!

She assumed she would eventually heal. It just would take some time. Eventually. After finals this week, she planned to go home to visit her parents before returning to good old Atlanta, Georgia to continue working at The Library and continue summer diving practice.

The Library Bar and Grill was where she saw Matt the first time. Her bartending job was actually great because she made excellent tips, and her boss, John Michaels, worked around her schedule. If it meant staying in Atlanta all summer to keep this job, she would. She just had to deal with the purgatory she was in right now. Matt couldn't promise he would return. Should she wait or go on with her life as her friends advised. She decided to give Matt time.

It would just take time.

Chapter 4

Her thoughts returned to her diving because a sophomore diver, Eric Walters, had already climbed up the board and accidentally brushed her arm.

"Hey, Domenica." He fist bumped her.

"Hey Eric," she responded.

He had to practice a new dive this week with a higher degree of difficulty. Before he continued talking to her, he perused the male swimmers and divers. Eric Walters was the only other person on the team who studied the male swimmers and divers' physiques more than she did! Going into a reverie, her brain suddenly relived the memory of the first day she met him last year:

"Fuckin' wow!" Domenica thought in shock as the new freshman diver just performed a Reverse Three and One-Half Somersaults platform dive to perfection. That was a three point four degree of difficulty! Damn! He surfaced, jumped out of the pool, and headed toward her. That's when she noticed the waterproof eyeliner and mascara on his eyelids and lashes. He gracefully extended his hand while he introduced himself. "Hi, I'm Eric. Eric Walters. You have to be Domenica Bartholomew. I've been following your career for about three years now. Didn't you place first in your state competitions?"

"Yes I did. You are quite amazing yourself. Do I know you from somewhere?"

"I'm in your physical education dance class, silly." He was shocked she didn't realize that. *"Lord, I can't believe you did not notice me in that class. I mean, just look at me."*

"Oh yes. Yes. Now I remember," she smiled, *"You are in my ballroom dancing class."*

Domenica thought about how colleges mandated so many hours of physical education for every student. Apparently, the institutions wanted each student to lead a healthy lifestyle, and five hours a week of some sort of activity for a semester evidently kept a person living forever! It didn't hurt that the tuition paid to the school for these <u>important</u> classes was always an added bonus.

All students knew that the object was to take a physical education class activity they'd already been doing their whole lives. For the first few weeks, they acted as though they were terrible at it. Miraculously, the students became the premiere athletes of the class by midterm because the college professors graded based on their improvement.

"Have you ever danced before?" she asked.

"Pa-lease! I actually teach ballroom dancing, but don't tell the prof."

"I won't cuz I've actually had about fourteen years of all kinds of dance myself. We should collaborate. I can see an A for the both of us."

"That's a great idea. Oh, and I just love your suit on you. That jade green color is one of my favorites." He quickly switched topics. *"So what's the lowdown on some of the guys around here? That one over there. Is he available?"* He asked this as he began to scope out Jason Lowry, the macho captain of the swim team who thought every woman wanted him. Apparently, ever man did too!

"Jason is only into the ladies, I'm afraid." Domenica chuckled to herself and thought she should have tried to fix Eric up with Jason just to watch Jason squirm.

"Oh well. His loss." Eric touched her hand, smiled, and headed for the platform again.

Domenica started her 3-meter climb, performed her dive, and felt good about it. She would have it down pat in a few days. Coach Jeffries critiqued both divers for another half an hour before he ended practice.

Walking out of the natatorium, Domenica bumped into Eric Walters again.

"Listen, do you have time to practice a dance routine in about an hour?" he asked her. I have the small practice basketball court signed out, so we could go over some stuff." He studied her by gliding up and down her body, then added, "Bring some type of dance outfit with you, if you have one, so I can find something to match. Maybe we can fit in a bit of a dress rehearsal too. I think a collaboration will deliver an A for both of us."

"I think I could arrange that. Meet you over there in a bit."

She ran back to her apartment and changed into something comfortable for dancing. Then, she collected her old competition dance ensemble she had her mom send from home just for this damn dance class. She was now on her way to the small gym.

Entering the gym, she recognized it as a place where the college kids could go for some one-on-one activities, such as basketball or volleyball. Domenica heard that a long time ago this was where the renowned Atlanta, Georgia Carlton State University basketball team officially played.

How the times had changed. The new facility was as huge as the professional teams' complexes. She was elated that this court was available to students for activities with friends without having to pay anything. She saw Eric in the back corner plugging in his iPhone into his portable Bluetooth speaker. She yelled loudly to him, "Are we doing a Latin number or a jitterbug?"

"Oh. Hi! I want to see your outfit, and then we can decide."

She pulled the plastic covering off the hanger that cradled her most beautiful and daring outfit. Eric's eyes glowed with envy. It was a long-sleeve, nude-colored leotard with sheer nude-colored fabric covering her arms and the low-cut back, so even though she was totally covered, she did not look covered—at all. Black lace appliqués covered in white sequences were strategically sewn over her chest, butt, and, let's just say, the down-there area. All of this was hidden under a black, silk robe fastened together with a wide, red satin tie that definitely accentuated her small waist, wide hips, and large bust.

"Wow, Domenica! Seeing you in this might even make me go straight!" Eric exclaimed. He now talked to himself aloud. "The prof is male and straight. Hmmm. It will work! I like it!" He turned to address Domenica with enthusiasm. "We are doing Latin steps, and do I have the song. It's a cover, and instead of the music starting first, the back-up singers will start first. I already arranged it. Hmm." He tapped his index finger over his lips. "We are going to need a chaise couch for you to sleep on. We can use that banquet table for a prop today.

She smiled and said, "Okay. Anything you say, Fred."

They sat on the floor and started to go over some Latin dance steps with some modern elements added. <u>Just like getting back on a bicycle,</u> she thought.

After about a half hour of practice, Eric said, "Go put your outfit on, and we can practice the part where I pull off the robe. I know we are looking at an A here, Ginger." He continued her reference to Fred Astaire and Ginger Rogers.

"I think so too, Fred," she laughed. She started to head toward the locker when she heard her name.

"Yo! Dommie-dog!" Dawan Owens called out. Jamal Jackson and he entered the gym with a basketball. The two players lived three doors down from Domenica and were involved

in helping Matt, devising a plan to help him escape by dressing him as a black student going to one of their away games. "You got ta go. We in here to practice today. Some one-on-one."

"Did you sign out the room?" she asked.

"We don't have to. Can't you see we basketball players?"

"I've watched you play, Dawan, so that is a subject up for debate," she teased.

They approached her trying to figure out what the two were doing.

Eric introduced himself to the two fine looking male studs and told them, "You should leave and let us finish, because the way she and I dance, you may have some trouble controlling your man parts, not that I would complain." His eyes drifted over both players.

Dawan just stared down at him. "We proud black men. We can control our man parts, little white boy."

"Do you want to place a bet on that, Dawan?" Domenica had to pipe in. "How about fifty dollars and us being able to finish our practice. Whoever loses pays up and leaves."

Dawan and Jamal looked at each other knowing they would easily win, and Jamal responded, "It's a bet, but you can only dance with Eric or in front of us, Domenica. You can't touch us."

"I wouldn't think of it. Let me go change. Eric, cue the music. I'll be right out. Dawan, when Eric tells you, hit the play button." She went into the locker to change while Eric moved the banquet table to the center of the floor as their prop. Next, he placed the two players a few feet away from it.

"This is gonna be an easy fifty." Jamal quietly said, slapping Dawan's hand. "I watched this ballroom dancing shit. Too high class for me, and nothing sexy about it. All planned and too prancy."

Domenica returned in her robe tied with a red sash, totally covered up. Under it was, of course, the outfit that turned gay men straight. She and Eric took their positions, Eric to the side and Domenica sleeping on the table. Eric nodded to Dawan. The music started.

"Wake up, wake up, wake up, Wake up…" the voices reverberated as the song "Sexual Healing" started to fill the gym.

Eric crossed over to Domenica, his hand gliding up the side of her supine body. She awakens and takes his hand. He lifts her from the table, and as he places her down into a split, he pulls the sash, grabs the sleeves, and pulls off the robe throwing it, as she performs a chaine turn to a jazz layout to the floor. She comes up into a sexy jazz walk back to Eric, her nude leotard highlighting her perfect physique. She and Eric perform a basic Corte. They flow into the Argentine dance of love, a tango, as Dawan stares at her.

"I'm out," Dawan whispered to Jamal. "It's all on you to win us the money, bro'." He walked to the bleachers and sat, putting his jacket over his lap to hide his rising interest in dance. His eyes became hooded watching Domenica dance.

They executed a few more tango steps. Then the couple gyrated to the floor with Eric rhythmically maneuvering his hips on top of her. As the song reverberated "…love tonight," they used their hips to bump and grind to the beat. She sat up to touch her forehead to his, as he gently touched the side of her face. From that point, he slid his hand down to her chin, then down the center of her body. Then he jumped up, lifted her up, and finally they continued with more tango steps. Still thinking about the fifty dollars, she broke free from Eric and danced to Jamal.

Never touching him, she performed intricate body rolls within a few inches of him, especially with her hips and butt. She met his eyes with hers, staring at him seductively as she danced in front of him with the illusion of her hand raised flat against his chest, but still a few inches from it. Her hand slowly descended down, quite near his man parts without touching him at all. Gracefully, she turned her body, thrust her hips out, and started to twerk, a move she learned from a New Orleans dancer.

Jamal jumped back. "Okay! Okay! You win! Fuck!" he yelled and went to sit by Dawan, who somberly whispered to him, as he handed Jamal his hoodie, "I'm switching my major from criminal justice to dance tomorrow!"

The two of them rose with Jamal slapping a fifty in her hand. He grabbed his shit, and walked out of the gym with Dawan.

Domenica quickly pulled out of her reverie smiling when Eric asked, "Listen up, girlfriend. Greg, Sal, and I are going to the dance studio to practice for competition tonight. Do you want to tag along?"

"You know what? That just might be what I need. Same time at seven?"

"Yes. We can go over some of our newer routines. I really want to pick up the USA title since we already took the state title."

After she and Eric performed in that college dance class last year, Domenica decided to return to ballroom dancing. With fourteen years of dance experience, going back to it now reminded her of how she could lose herself in the art of dance. When she danced, she would simply turn off her brain for a while, leaving only her soul to take control of her body. She felt it meld with the air around her, turning her body into fluid movement. She needed this to forget, even if it was for the moment. Besides, with just work and diving during the summer months, she had time on her hands, something she did not want to deal with.

Of course, Domenica really liked the competition part of it too, since she and Eric were winning every title that came into their paths. Let's face it. They were both gymnasts turned divers turned dancers. There was not one lift, drop, twist, or dip they could not do to perfection. For her, this was competition for fun.

The same semester that she danced with Eric, he set everything up for her to meet Kevin Bellamy, the owner of the ballroom dance studio. Kevin was kind enough to let her practice and perform with the male instructors there for free. However, his generous actions were not without benefit to him. She was eye-candy on his male dancers' arms. She knew the steps, lifts, dips, twists, and drops. Her perfect gymnastics skills rivaled no one, as did her perfect physique. She would be an added bonus in competition with other studios and in the national and international arenas. He was looking at making a name for his studio, and she and Eric would be the ones to put him on the map. Oh yes, he was *so* generous.

Domenica and Eric had already won the district and state competition title for best male/female ballroom dancers. In four weeks, they were competing for the USA title. Their dance was the Paso Doble. Eric had to throw her up in the air where she would do a twist and come down in his arms.

She now had little free time to think about Matt. That was reserved for when she was alone, with just her memories and shattered heart. "Okay then. I will see you at seven tonight."

Chapter 5

The venue for the USA ballroom dance competitions occurred at the Plaza Hotel in downtown Atlanta this year. Only the best of the best attended to compete, the ones who won their state competitions. Domenica and Eric were in the running after they took their state competition title about a month ago. Both were happy that they didn't even have to travel as many of the other couples had done. None of their daily routines changed in any way, which was extremely advantageous. Kevin's dance studio and dancers hosted the event, managing all of the night's festivities.

The announcer began, "Ladies and gentlemen, Eric Walters and Domenica Bartholomew, our last couple of the evening and representing the beautiful state of Georgia, are performing the Paso Doble."

The lights and the applause dimmed simultaneously as Eric took her hand. When their selected song began to play, the classic "*Maraguena*," they glided onto the dance floor.

Eric whispered so only she could hear. "The rest of them simply don't have a chance. Let's show them what perfection is."

Domenica smiled as they started their first movement. She knew he was correct in his assumption. With his and her athletic and dance abilities, the judges watched two people flawlessly dance from step to step. They witnessed perfect dips, lifts, and drops. Their musicality was synonymous with the song, gliding into gentle moves or jerking to the staccato riffs in the bridge of the song. It helped that both Eric and Domenica were flawless in their appearances too, donning bodies of elite gymnasts. Just as they became one with the diving board, these two became one with the song and dance floor, two people working as a single, fluid motion. The audience cheered at many of their dangerous drops and lifts.

Not cheering, but also seated in the audience, was Kade Abraham, who easily researched and found Domenica Bartholomew. He had been tailing her for weeks trying to learn her habitual daily routines and hangouts. With the help of the Colonel, he knew more about her than she knew about herself. She was a natural-born beauty, Italian decent, athletically gifted, and based on her transcripts, quite intelligent. She also appeared to be an innocent in the ways of the world, a product of a small town where people cared for each other and trusted each other. He would use that to his advantage.

As far as his investigation so far, she'd had no recent contact with Matt Hoover. In fact, she seemed to have gotten over him rather quickly with a Jamal somebody, even though that relationship did not last long. Probably a rebound.

However, as a red-blooded American male, what he was most impressed with was her physical shape. In his line of work, he had been with a lot of one night stands when he'd had his urges, and most of the women were aesthetically beautiful or physically delightful, but rarely was any woman both drop-dead gorgeous, the perfect specimen of feminine physical beauty and intelligence. She was the poster child of what a perfect woman should be, if there was such a creature.

And, yes, he was going to enjoy investigating Domenica Bartholomew.

And, yes, he was going to fuck her.

What the Colonel didn't know wouldn't hurt him. He would be plowing into that fertile field by at least the second date. Count on it!

He looked back at the dance floor and realized the emcee was about to announce the winning couple, not that he cared. His eyes constantly perused her up and down. This was going to be the best assignment ever—and he would be paid a lot of money to boot.

"And the winning couple is…" The announcer paused to create tension. Then, he shouted out the two names. "Eric Walters and Domenica Bartholomew from the State of Georgia!"

Eric screamed and jumped up and down more than Domenica did! Once again, she was doing this for a pastime, not concerned if she won anything at all. The other dance instructors from the studio ran up to them to hug and congratulate them. Greg Andrews and Salvatore Costa pounded on Eric's back while another dancer handed Domenica a dozen roses.

"We've got to go and celebrate!" Sal was always into partying.

Eric agreed. "Yes, let's go to that new place, *Hook Up Here.*"

"Hook up here?" Domenica began to laugh hysterically. "Why? Are people now having trouble hooking up at bars on their own, so they have to explicitly have a place to go?"

"Hey. I can hook up anywhere!" Greg retaliated.

"Come on, Domenica. Don't be a party pooper. Please? Please? Please, please, please?"

"Oh, all right. We can go there to celebrate. I haven't been to a club in a long time. But none of you had better leave me, cuz I'm not hooking up with anyone!"

They started for the door.

Walking a few steps behind was Kade Abraham who would get to Grandma's house before Little Red Riding Hood. Finally, a perfect place to meet his secondary mission, Domenica Bartholomew.

***

An hour later, Sal directed his question to Domenica who was already pushing past everyone in the line to see if the bouncer would direct her little group into the club. "Do you think we can get in here tonight?"

"If we can't make the cut into the club dressed in these outfits, we'll never get in."

She was referring to their attire. They'd just come from the ballroom dance competition and never even changed out of their outfits. Domenica was in a form-fitting, red lace dress, if one could call it that. It was backless down to almost her butt crack—not that hers looked like a plumber's butt crack—with every defined muscle of her back on display for all to see. The hemline was uneven with one side crawling up to her hip showing off her black fishnet stockings, while her fuck-me-red glitter platforms clung to her feet by thick black ribbons tied at the ankles. The other side of the dress, on her opposite hip, floated down to her ankle. The uneven hemline guided a man's eye to glide from the bottom of her muscular legs to the top of her hip, a pleasurable place for a man to sojourn. Yes that "eyejourn" was most pleasurable. In front, the dress was also low enough to see her ample ba-sooms that she could not hide even if her life depended on it.

Domenica Bartholomew was not only a ballroom dancer, as of tonight, she was now the best in the USA, or so her ribbons and medals said. Now competing in Europe? That was a different story. A lot of excellent competition lived over there. Be that as it may, tonight—over here—she was the queen bee.

Her three companions, all dance instructors at the studio, became her best dance friends ever since she went back into dancing in Atlanta. Her diving teammate Eric Walters, Greg Andrews, and Salvatore Costa were just crazy. She loved hanging with them because no other male approached her to hit on her while she was out just to have a good time. Besides, it was like going out with the girls, since all three were gay, though the only one who acted that way was Eric. He walked like a girl, talked like a girl, dressed in flashy colors and his hand gestures were to die for. Sometimes she thought he purposely advertised his gayness as if to say, "This is what I am. Different, but oh, so much better!"

Greg always wore clothes from a GQ cover: hair perfect, skin perfect, glasses perfect, walk perfect, and body perfect. When they went out, people would look at him and just wonder if he was or not.

Then there was Sal Costa, an Italian skin tone, piercing dark, sexy eyes, and black, black hair. Anyone could tell he worked out. He looked like an NFL receiver at about six foot four with an amazingly proportioned body. No one would ever have guessed that he was gay. He looked and acted like the typical jock.

Not that all the males who danced ballroom were gay, but straight men would hit on her when she just wanted friends, not boyfriends. After Matt disappeared, Domenica did not date. She had only been with him for about six months, but he was her other half. She did not go out looking for another other half.

The day she saw him boarding the bus, she decided she would not betray his love. She should have gone with him, but no. God made her stay to endure empty day after empty day. Sometimes she wondered what she did so wrong in her life to be given such a punishment as losing half of her soul.

She slyly lifted her girls up higher so that her cleavage was up and center. She approached the bouncer. She figured that if she wasn't his type, she would send Sal up to try. "Any way my friends and I could get in?" she asked smiling innocently glancing up through her long, dark lashes, although he never noticed the smile or the flirting lashes. His eyes drifted right to where she expected them to drift.

"Sure. You and your friends come on through, angel." He looked around for the other beautiful girls accompanying her. "Where are your friends?"

Domenica was already through with Greg, Eric, and Sal in pursuit. "Right here," she exclaimed as all four entered into the hottest dance club in Atlanta, maybe even the whole state of Georgia. "Thanks."

Chapter 6

Hook-Up Here was definitely true to its name. If anyone wanted to find a hook-up for the night, all he or she had to do was get into this three-story club. Its tall ceilings gave the place a massive feel. On any given night that it was open, it was nothing to see eight hundred to a thousand people sitting at the three bars placed on the different levels, dancing on huge dance floors, sitting in the conversational couch areas and at tables, or just chilling with a drink. These people all had the same goal: to find someone for long-term or just for the night. Domenica was probably the only one there just to let herself get lost in dance, so she could forget the haunting water-colored memories that opaquely smeared over her brain.

"Here's a table," Eric pointed out. "It's right at the edge of the dance floor." They all sat and looked around to become acquainted with their surroundings. "God, this is really amazing!" Eric said, surprised at the ambiance the place exuded.

"I'm going to buy us some drinks. What does everybody want?" Sal listened for their orders.

"Beer," Eric answered quickly.

"Martini," Greg yelled over the table.

"Just get me Kahlua and cream," Domenica called out as she studied the place.

"No wonder it is the hot spot of Atlanta. We arrived here early; and there are a lot of people dancing already."

Greg shook his head in agreement. "If we would have waited until the time everyone starts to go out, we might not have made it in because of the building code count. I already feel like a sardine packed in a tin can."

She now noticed that Eric went up to hit on the DJ, apparently slipping him a piece of paper with his phone number on it.

Sal and Eric both returned to their table together. The four of them enjoyed their first round, still checking out the people who were entering by the truckloads. A server finally approached their table and took their orders for round two.

Suddenly Michael Jackson's "Billy Jean" echoed throughout the room. Domenica now knew what was on that paper, some of Eric's favorite dance tunes.

Eric jumped up swaying his hips to the music and then reached out for Domenica's hand. "Come on, girlfriend. Let's show off our cha-cha."

She smiled taking his hand, and they gracefully moved to the floor, competition-style. Then, he pulled her into a lift over his shoulders spinning her around his neck to a dead drop to the floor.

"There," he said to her as he lifted her up, "No one will dare come out now to compete with us for the dance floor."

He was so right. They became the center of attraction on the dance floor to a mesmerized audience. People actually started to group around the floor to watch the two as they danced, no holds barred.

Of course, one set of eyes only watched Domenica.

When that song ended, the DJ went right into Gloria Estefan's "Rhythm is Gonna Get You" with Greg sauntering to them. He cut in taking Domenica's hand while Eric went to his seat to down yet another drink.

"You know I have to outshine Eric, girlfriend." He led her right into a salsa. Everyone was oohing and aahing when they performed various lifts and dips. She was lost in the dance.

She recognized the next song as En Vogue's "My Lovin' (You're Never Gonna Get It)." She also glanced at Eric finishing Greg's martini as Sal danced out to the floor to take this song.

"My turn to show you off," he said to her smiling as he moved into place.

They flowed from salsa into an Argentine Tango, the war of the legs. With Sal's and her Mediterranean background, they flowed into the sultry moves, dancing sensuously across the floor. Everyone started to hoot and holler at some of the suggestive moves, especially when they rubbed up against each other, literally, almost dry humping. Domenica looked like steaming hot melted caramel sex on a platter as she moved her hips and legs to the beat of the music. All the men watching certainly noticed the delectable treat. It was as though she became the rhythm of the song, all the while looking at Sal with those "never gonna get it" eyes.

Finally, Dr. Dre's "No Diggity" honed into the blend. Eric quickly downed another drink as he sauntered out again to dance to the sexy song. Sal placed Domenica's hand into his and went to sit down.

"I'm baaaack," he almost sang out.

"Eric! You okay?" Domenica sensed that something was wrong right away.

"I'm great!" Eric started to lead but something was off. He was losing his equilibrium and rhythm to the music.

She started to worry as he led her into all those spins and turns. She tried to control the dance moves, but he fought her and started to lead again.

Then, the catastrophe.

He maneuvered her over to the edge of the dance floor and lifted her up over his head. He was supposed to balance her on his shoulders in her standing position and then throw her into the air, from there catching her in his arms. But this drunken ass could not even walk, let alone find his position to catch someone! He flipped her up high, but lost his balance and started to fall back.

As he tossed her up in the air, panic struck Domenica when she felt him sway away from her. "Eric!"

Paying attention to him instead of her aerial twist, she lost her direction in the movement and started to fall to the hard floor. In those few seconds, all she could think of was, *Don't hit your head. Don't hit your head. Tuck! Tuck!*

In the next millisecond, Eric was flat on the floor and she was...

"Whoa! Gotcha!"

...in the arms of this tall, dark, mysterious stranger who apparently jumped up from his front table to catch her!

The room disappeared; the people disappeared; the noise disappeared; the lights disappeared; everything vanished—except him. The two of them were alone in an alternate dimension.

He had her wrapped tightly in his arms and was staring into her hypnotizing eyes, while she gazed at his face. And what a face it was!

Those piercing blue—or were they platinum—eyes. Deep. Penetrating. Suggestive. If a person could fuck with his eyes to bring a woman to climax, he was doing just that to her in this moment. She thought he might be in his late twenty's, early thirty's. She certainly could feel every muscle in his chest as he held her closer into him.

She had never seen a man so perfect in her life, as though the Divine Hand sculpted him. Otherworldly. Richard Gere, Brad Pitt, George Clooney, Michele Marrone, and Sean Connery all rolled up into one sexmonstration of what a flawless man should be.

Of course, sometimes Lucifer sends temptation disguised in a flawless gift package—or in sky blue eyes that can truly tranquilize.

It was only then that she remembered Matt.

Chapter 7

Just as the dance club's name implied, Kade Abraham was at *Hook-Up Here* to try, nonchalantly, to meet Domenica. He also figured while he was here, he would pick up an easy lay for the night if things didn't work out with her. He watched the young woman dancing on the floor wondering if she could demonstrate those same moves while he was fucking her. Her body was magnificent. That long dark, curly hair hung loosely down her defined back and flitted over her breasts. They were huge, every man's fantasy. Her long legs had that same defined muscle tone that he saw on her back. That ass? Round and toned. How the hell much body fat could she have? She must have lived in a weight room. She. Was. Exquisite.

He could not get over his luck as he saw an accident waiting to happen with her drunken asshole dance partner. He stood quickly thinking that he would just grab her when they tripped, but for this idiot to try a lift with her in his condition and then lose his balance? This was bad. He waited for the inevitable.

He did not have to wait long before he witnessed her partner heave her high up into the air and then trip back with Domenica falling, falling—into Kade's waiting arms. *Thanks God,* he thought as he caught her quickly drawing her body into him.

"Whoa! Gotcha!"

Then he looked into her eyes. He could not stop staring at her face. With his lips slightly parted in stunned amazement, he continued his gaze upon her as though he ensnared a mystical creature that people only read about. Was it a second? A minute? An hour? How long did she have him transfixed? He clung to her as she returned the mesmerized stare.

And then finally,

"Umm. Could you take your hand off my boob?" Domenica was the first to return to reality, finally noticing this man's hand was pressing into her right breast. It was how his one hand caught and held onto her as she fell. The other thankfully hooked under her bent knees.

"What?" He returned to the present too, not sure of what he thought he heard.

"My breast? You have your hand clutched into my breast." She threw her head back in a chuckle and added, "Is this how you've been trained to save women in distress?"

Embarrassed, he quickly put her down on one foot first, removing his wayward hand. "Oh! God! Um…Yes I do!" He then wryly uttered in her ear. "I thought that might have been my reward for saving your life." He smiled deviously at her as he stood her up on both feet. "Really though, I am sorry. I just hung on to you any way I could. After I caught you. So both of us wouldn't go down. Because I …" He was stuttering. "I do apologize again, although I've enjoyed every minute of holding your breast… Umm…in my hand…for a long length of time." His lips curved into that devilish smile. Then he whispered in her ear, "I *could* put my hand somewhere else. Somewhere warm."

Domenica smiled at his remark, but instantly turned serious. "I do want to thank you for your quick reaction. I could have been seriously hurt if not for you. I guess I won't be too upset over your holding my breast…in your hand…for a long length of time." She returned the devilish smile reiterating his phrases with the same pauses.

"Any time you want to try that again just let me know, and I'll be there." Then, he leaned into her, kissed her forehead, and whispered in her ear again. "Or if you need someone just to hold your breast! I'm the breast man for the job!" His laughter was very contagious.

"Yes. You. Are." She liked the thought of him being her man. *Think of Matt. Think of Matt.*

"And I think I now qualify in the breast-holding department, in case the need ever would arise again." He leered down at her with that same mesmerizing grin.

"Well, um, thanks again for saving me. I've got to get back to my friends."

"And thank you. You know…for letting me hold your breast." Neither realized they were still holding hands while their conversation occurred. He quickly dropped his hand from hers, and she walked away from him.

Back to her table…On the other side of the dance floor…Stumbling a few times…With people on the floor…Hiding her from his view.

Damn! Kade watched her maneuver through the floor of dancing people. "Did I capture her, or did she just capture me?" he said quietly to himself. And how was he going to take advantage of meeting her like this. He knew he could not seem too anxious.

As she sat at her table, Domenica reached over and smacked Eric on the head. "I could have been seriously hurt out there, you idiot! And I *will* be driving home."

"A minor mishap, guuurlfriend," he slurred. "And pray tell. Who the hell is that hot guy?"

"I don't know. I did not get his name nor did he ask for mine."

"And you are going to leave it at that? That hotty? The one who saved your life? Did you at least thank him?"

"Yes, I said thank you."

"No, I mean *really* thank him, like buy him a drink or, better yet, go over and dance with him."

"Oh. I didn't think of that." She glanced over at him as Kade lifted his glass to her, smiling that mischievously devilish grin. "Hmm, I don't know."

"Your problem is you think too much. March your fucking ass over there right now." Eric sounded like her father commanding her to do the right thing.

"You need to move on, Domenica," Sal added not mentioning Matt's name aloud. "How long are you going to wait for someone who is no longer around?"

Maybe he was right. All these months and not one word, not one attempt to make contact. Now, it was the summer with the school year about to start in late August. Maybe *he* moved on, maybe he could never come back. He had certainly left her in limbo.

Chapter 8

Her thoughts and vision returned to this Adonis. She could have been injured seriously, but this man's quick thinking prevented a disaster from happening. She stood up, straightened her dress, and marched through the dancers to his table.

As she extended her hand, she introduced herself. "I am so sorry. I should have introduced myself to you. I am Domenica Bartholomew, and I would like to maybe buy you a drink?" She then noticed his full glass wondering if it was a foolish idea to suggest another drink. She also checked his hands for a wedding ring. Nope!

He stood and reached to shake her extended hand as he smiled softly. "Hmmm. Domenica Bartholomew. Are you the diver who wins all the titles that the AJC covers in its sports section all the time?"

"Um, yes. That's me."

"Those articles stated that you might try out for the Olympics."

"Well, those articles are wrong. College competition is bad enough."

He motioned for her to sit down on the chair beside his. "By the way, I am good on the drinks. I am Kade Abraham. Are any of those men at your table your boyfriend? Or fiancé? Or husband? Or a friend with benefits? Because I would like to ask you to dance this slow song with me, but I don't want to step on any toes." He arched one eyebrow up as he grinned at her again hoping she caught his humorous double meaning.

She did. She responded with a smile as her body melted. "Just friends and mostly my dance partners. I'm involved in competitive ballroom dancing among other things." She took his hand as he led her to the floor.

He turned to her and pulled her close encapsulating her into his body—again.

She felt like a butterfly in its protective Kade Abraham cocoon. In the background, Michael Bolton's "When a Man Loves a Woman" echoed through the building.

"Please do not compare me to your friends. I know how to move around on a dance floor, but you and your friends just put everyone in here to shame." Kade pulled her in closer. God, her body felt amazing so close to his. He had to control his dick, because it definitely had a mind of its own. She nestled into him. Her eyes drifted up to his, and he wondered if she could see or even sense his desire. Damn, she was heaven, and he wanted to have access to those pearly gates.

He had to admit the old colonel was correct. She certainly could make any man lose his way. He had planned how he would meet her, but this was just perfect. Christ, he just saved her life—practically. Now, all he had to do was to gain her trust. Of course, he would have to take on a very different persona, because he didn't want to scare her away. He would be the perfect gentleman. It was certainly a new persona for him. At least he would try. Old dog, new tricks—especially in dealing with women.

"Would you like to go with me to have a cup of coffee? I know a little café not far from here. I really don't want this night to end just yet. You know. Fate and all." His platinum-beamed eyes lasered through hers.

Domenica looked at her friends still downing drinks. "Well, I don't..."

"We can tell your friends where we are going. I'll even leave one of my business cards with them, if that makes you feel more comfortable."

"Um. That's..." Sal's advice, to get back out there, echoed in her mind. "Yes. Thank you. We can do that." They danced over to Eric's table. "I'm going with Kade for coffee."

"Kade Abraham," He introduced himself to Sal, Greg, and Eric shaking their hands and explaining that Domenica and he were leaving. "Here's my business card to get in touch with me if needs arise. I won't keep her out too late." He looked into her eyes and smiled. Of course, he would.

"Just remember that we are her big brothers down here, if anyone tries any funny business." Sal entered Kade's personal space as he stated that fact. Kade just thought about how quickly he could kill Sal, twisting his head around with a snap, breaking his neck. They had no idea who they were dealing with, and he would keep it that way.

"Believe me. I will be the perfect gentleman."

After they said their good-byes, he led Domenica out to valet service, and they waited for his car. "So when did you start dancing?"

"When I was about four years old. My mom put my sister and me into dance and gymnastics." She left out the karate part, just in case. "Both of us just loved it. We used to tumble around the house. And when music was on, we became back up dancers jumping all over the place."

A silver Porsche stopped in front of them with the valet jumping out. Domenica looked at Kade with those 'this-is-yours?' eyes.

"The real-estate business is rather lucrative." He responded to her with fake humility.

"I guess so!"

He opened her door and closed it when she settled into the car. Then he walked around, slid in, and again noticed her beauty as the city lights caressed her face. Damn, he was going to have to practice control with this one.

"So you are a real estate agent here in Georgia?"

"Actually, I'm a licensed agent here, in Florida, New York, and in Nevada where I have other offices."

The car purred down the street, turning around the corner to a bistro-type coffee house. He stopped in front of the valet, went around to open her door, but the valet was already helping her out, checking her over as he admired her long, defined legs stretched out onto the pavement.

Kade watched the young man check out her cleavage too, deciding that he would assassinate this young valet free of charge. He pulled her away from the young man's wandering eyes and gruffly barked, "Thank you. I can take it from here." He moved in close to Domenica, his hand on her lower back guiding her to a small u-shaped booth in the back, away from all the bustle.

"Is this good?"

"Perfect." She smiled at him, warming his very core when he slid in right next to her.

Yes, he was going to have to control the connection he felt with her. The server interrupted them with a menu asking the usual, their beverage for the evening.

"I think I'd like a French Vanilla Cappuccino."

"Just a plain coffee. Black. And that is all, unless you want something from the menu, Domenica?"

She studied it, but was satisfied with just the coffee.

"So how is it you don't have a boyfriend or fiancé or husband or a friend with benefits? I mean, girls like you get snatched up pretty quick."

Domenica wondered if she could get through talking about Matt. "I actually just broke up with my boyfriend, or should I say, he broke up with me. We met last fall. I thought he was amazing. He was kind, good, loving. He worked as a computer analyst, but he travelled so much." She looked down at her clasped hands, took a breath, and looked back up at Kade. "I think he finally realized it couldn't work. I don't know what went wrong. I just. He broke up with me in a letter. How about that. I gave him everything, and he gave me a letter saying it wasn't working out. And I don't want to talk about this anymore." Domenica realized she was becoming emotional, so she quickly looked down, blinked a few times, and then just fiddled with her hands.

"Wow! A letter. I'm sorry Domenica. I didn't think… I mean, I was just asking." Kade started to keep mental notes on what she knew. So far, she only thought he was a computer analyst with apparently no idea he worked for an OGA.

"It's alright, Kade. That's why I don't have a boyfriend or fiancé or husband or a friend with benefits. How about you? Why don't you have someone? You are quite ethereal."

"Ethereal?" Kade actually blushed at this remark. "God, I never heard *that* one before."

"Yes, ethereal. Of course, so was the fallen angel Lucifer." She smiled coyly, batting those dark lashes deviously at him.

"Oh, many who know me think I'm the Devil…Hmmm, ethereal…" He liked that she thought he was otherworldly. "Oh, I've dated. When I was younger, I had a girlfriend for a few months, but she wanted one thing, and I wanted her and my freedom. Oh, and other women! I definitely wanted other women too. That didn't work out so well."

Domenica laughed at his comment. Kade looked into her eyes and added, "I just never found anyone to peak my interests. That is until maybe tonight." He looked at her and placed his hand over her hands as his thigh touched hers. *She did not pull back. Good to know.*

"Wait! Did I peak your interest or did the peak of my boob peak your interest?" She might have had a few too many drinks tonight also.

Kade's laughter was loudly robust as he almost spewed his mouthful of coffee forward.

As people around them looked to see what the commotion was all about, he answered, "I'm going to plead the fifth on that one."

Smiling, Domenica was now studying his face. "You look like you have a Greek ethnicity."

"And you are very observant. My mother was Greek and my father French. So I do resemble my mother. The eyes are my dad's."

"Well, I'm mostly Italian. Oh, and a little Spanish in me."

Kade leaned over rubbing his cheek against hers as he whispered in her ear, "I could arrange for you to have a little *Greek* in you." That devilish smile was on display again.

Without missing a beat, Domenica countered back. "I hope the definitive word in that statement is not *little*."

Chapter 9

Kade's brusque laughter disrupted the people around them again, with one older couple instantly perusing them with an irritated look. "Absolutely not! I'm great in that department."

"Larger than your ego?"

He had to laugh again. "You are talented and intelligent and quite funny." Now he stared at her. "Look, Domenica, let me be blunt. I would like to go out on a date with you. How about tomorrow? Maybe see where this might go." He raised his hand and pointed back and forth between the two of them adding, "Because there is definitely a connection of some sort here. At least for me."

"Oh wow! You *do* come right to the point." She returned seriously.

"I believe in letting everyone know where I stand in any situation."

Her thoughts shifted to Matt, about waiting for him. She had barricaded the door to her heart so tight that not even the big, bad wolf could blow it down and destroy it again.

However, a person cannot live barricaded in a safety zone forever. She had to emerge from that safe haven at some point. Would it really hurt to go out with ethereal Kade a few times? This attraction she felt just might fizzle in a few dates. She had to push herself to abandon the safe room once again, to experience life and maybe even love. "I guess a date wouldn't hurt."

Kade's face looked like the rising sun on an early summer morning. "Okay then." He clapped his hands together. "Where would the most beautiful woman in the world like to go first?"

"How about we just start out with dinner or maybe a movie?"

Or a date in my bed. That feeling one has when he achieves a goal? It permeated through Kade's pores for the rest of the evening. They talked and laughed for a few more hours before Domenica told him she had to go home. Always the gentleman, Kade helped her from her chair and escorted her out of the café.

Back in his car as he drove her home, Domenica had to remove his hand from her leg a few times, especially when it started to rise up her thigh. And although she professed he did not have to walk her all the way to her apartment door, Kade did.

"I guess this is goodnight. Oooor... you could invite me in for maybe coffee, or drinks, or hell, I'll even take sex! That's if you have it!" He leaned into her and nuzzled his nose into her hair, smelling her sweet natural scent, his lips brushing her cheek.

"Um, I think tonight ends right at this door, Kade. I had an amazing time with you tonight. You made me happy." Then she added an afterthought. "Something I haven't been in a while."

"Oh, I could make tonight unforgettable, if you let me in!"

Christ! Even his husky tone is a major turn-on. Her girly parts started to become alive.

He closed in on her as he guided her body into the door. He leaned down and pressed his lips to hers. The kiss was light at first, but as she reciprocated, he started to lose control as his hands went back around her waist and down to her full, firm ass.

Fuck, he started to get hard. Still, she gave no resistance. He deepened the kiss, and his tongue parted her lips to gently brush against her tongue. Hands still on her ass, he pulled her deeper into him.

Fuck, I don't want to fight him. Domenica clasped her arms around his neck and floated her hands through that black, thick hair.

She could feel his dick pressing into her. Nope. *Little* was not the situation at all. She wanted to take him to her bed and use him to forget Matt.

Oh my God, Matt! She quickly pulled away from Kade. "Kade, stop." She gasped for air.

He did not stop. Who the hell ever said stop to Kade Abraham? He tried to deepen the kiss more.

"Stop!" This time she pushed hard against that defined chest.

Kade pulled back and stared, examining in deep concentration every detail of her face. Then, in his most seductive voice he whispered, "I could get lost in you, Domenica. And you could get lost in me. Let me come in."

The fallen angel tempted her in a low, sexy voice, and she almost gave in to him—almost.

"Kade, I just got out of a serious relationship. I can't, I just…" She turned from him and opened the door. As she slid through the opening, he grabbed her arm.

"We can take it slow. Just give me a chance. Okay?"

"Okay. Slow." She turned and closed the door as she called out to him. "Goodnight Kade. I really did enjoy myself tonight."

***

"This is the guy you met last week?" Shannon sounded like Domenica's mother already.

"Yes."

"So what time is he picking you up" Shannon appeared as nervous as Domenica, as she stared out the window watching for his Porsche.

"He'll be here in about ten minutes."

"You said he was thirty?" Shannon still watched out for the car.

"Thirty-one."

"You know older guys expect things and—"

"God. You sound just like my mother!" Domenica finally yelled at her.

"Hey! I just know you are still not over Matt, and I don't want you to get hurt again. He's here!" She shrieked out the last statement as she flew to the door. Domenica started to wonder who was more excited over this date. *Shannon*, she thought.

Domenica watched the TV monitor over her apartment door and saw him walk into the building like the king who had just conquered this territory. A slight shiver passed through her body. They had already gone out for a lunch date in the middle of the week, and tonight he said he had a surprise dinner date.

This new dating relationship with Kade was not like the one with Matt. With Matt, she felt comfortable, like they grew up together. He was the quiet summer day.

With Kade?

Kade was the thunderstorm that terrorized the quiet of the day. He was the epitome of what women fantasized about, the man that romantic novels depicted as an abstract of every other male on the planet. A Greek god come to life. Tall, gorgeous, muscular, physically perfect in his six-foot frame—and dominant, very dominant in his personality.

He physically made it known that he wanted her with kisses and touches and even with words. His words echoed in her ears again. *"I believe in letting everyone know where I stand in any situation."* He pushed her limits both times they were together. It was as though she had to constantly control a wild animal—and it was thrilling.

And yet, he was this fresh baked baklava just pulled from the oven, layered in romance mysteries, and filled with cinnamon-covered walnut bliss that was honey-coated in conflict. He tasted like perversity in its most wonderfully sensual form, an addicting cocaine and heroin cocktail splashed with a side of LSD, leading to the great pleasures or greater despair.

But for now this early in the game, he was the man who thrilled her with trepidation, because she never knew if he was going to be something good in her life or the worst disaster that could happen to all of humanity.

Kade. Was he an incubus or redeemer?

Even all of this didn't accurately describe Kade Abraham to his fullest.

Maybe with a few more dates she would find out.

She opened the door before he rang the buzzer and stepped to the side as he walked in. "Kade, this is Shannon Mavis. My friend I told you about. She lives above me. Shannon Mavis, Kade Abraham."

He stepped into her, and as he pulled her to him, he place a light kiss on her forehead. "Hi, Shannon. So you are the *other* friend?"

"That's me." Shannon was already lost in him, her eyes held captive by his.

God, this man, Domenica thought as she watched how he bewitched Shannon.

"I'm taking Domenica to dinner, and we might be back very late."

"Shannon, I *will* be back by midnight." Domenica sounded adamant about this.

Chapter 10

"Isn't this the café we went to the night we met?"

Kade drove past the café and turned into the underground parking garage. "Yes, it is. But we are not dining in the café. He parked his car in a reserved bay, walked around, and opened the door for her. She looked at him quizzically, and in return, he waggled his brows as he walked her to the elevator. After they entered, he put a key into the panel and punched fifteen.

"Kade? Where are we going?"

"To my place on the top floor."

"The penthouse?"

"Um, yes. Actually, I own the whole building, so I had Ramón, the chef from the café, cook us something light for dinner." He turned into her and pressed a kiss to her full lips.

"Just dinner?"

"Just dinner." He pressed his lips into hers again and then added, "And maybe a little dessert."

"Kade. I suggest you remember the definition of the word *slow*." Domenica turned away from him quite perturbed.

"Come on, Domenica." He pulled back from her. "I *am* going slow—for me." He accented the words *for me.* "I just thought we could talk through dinner. You know, learn more about each other and not be bothered by noise. Then if you want, we can watch a movie."

"Just so there are no expectations."

"No expectations."

The elevator buzzed to a stop. Domenica's eyeballs almost popped out of her head as she entered the massive foyer right off the elevator. A rectangular, mirrored table was centered in the foyer below a modern crystal chandelier. A centerpiece of beautiful, live flowers decorating the black ceramic vase they bathed in was its focal point. She walked into an open-concept living-dining-kitchen area. The color combinations were definitely Kade—very masculine. Grays, blacks and deep burgundy. Thoroughly modern décor.

"Let me show you around." Kade led her to the back bedroom. "This is where all of the magic happens." Kade roguishly smiled as he pointed to his massive four-poster bed. While they walked through the rest of the three-bedroom, two-bathroom penthouse, Domenica realized it was bigger than her parents' home.

"I guess the real-estate business *is* rather lucrative!" She was, indeed, impressed.

After the tour, he grabbed her hand and escorted her through a door off the kitchen. They walked up twelve steps and walked out onto a tropical paradise. The rooftop of the building was a finished terrace with plants, furniture, potted trees, twinkle lighting, and grass!

"Oh my God! It's beautiful!"

"I'm glad you approve. I designed this myself. Sometimes, I have parties up here for my clients. Tonight, it is just you and me." He waggled his brows again and led her to a small bistro table already set for dinner and helped her to sit down. "Ramon?" he called out.

"I'm back here." A voice resounded from behind the door by the small bar. Suddenly, a short, chubby Latino-looking man emerged with two salads, placing one in front of each of them.

The salad consisted of pieces of watermelon chunks, tomato wedges, avocado slices, and chickpeas, all placed on a bed of the greenest lettuce Domenica had ever seen. "The dressing is my own recipe, a pineapple vinaigrette. I hope you like it. For the main course, Mr. Kade asked for steak, but you, my dear, can order the steak or a chicken, salmon, shrimp, or pork entrée." He politely waited for her decision.

Domenica just stared at Kade. This was the most romantic setting she had ever experienced. "I think I will try the salmon. Thank you, Ramon."

"I will return with your main entrées in about twenty minutes." Winking at Kade, he left through another elevator door that Domenica assumed led right back down to the café kitchen.

"Wow! You pulled out the big guns tonight." Domenica did not wait for Kade to respond, because she was too busy scrutinizing the tropical paradise.

"I aim to please. You seem to like it." Kade started into his salad, and Domenica followed suit. "So did your old boyfriend ever call to apologize?"

Silence sounded as Domenica stopped eating to stare up at Kade. He knew instantly that she went into a defensive mode. *Too soon, too soon. I'm such a dumb fuck.*

"No one has called. Why would that interest you?" Domenica was on guard.

"I just...well, I... Look, Domenica, I seriously want to date you. But like you, and for the first time in my life, I don't want to get hurt. I think you understand that. I just want to know if there's a chance for me, before I am emotionally involved."

Domenica picked up her napkin and dabbed the side of her mouth. "I told you before that we will take this slow. I cannot and will not promise you anything else. I will also tell you that I enjoy your company and can't wait to see you when you are not near me. But! I will not rush into anything ever again. I'm sorry if I am not where you apparently are in our *very young* dating relationship." She stressed her words very young while she studied his face.

Kade recognized he just turned his fiasco into a quick save. She thought he was talking about their new relationship, when he really was probing for information about Matt. *Think. Think fast.* "Well, I told you I'm all about being up front. How about if I don't mention where this relationship is heading, and how about we both steer clear of topics like old boyfriends and girlfriends."

"I would appreciate that immensely."

"Good. Shall we continue with our dinner?" Kade stabbed his fork back into his salad, grateful for his quick turnaround.

The music changed to another romantic love song. Ed Sheeran's voice floated around them as he sang "Thinking Out Loud."

"I love this song," Domenica sighed.

"Then we should dance to it." Kade stood and reached for her hand. He didn't ask. He just waited until she finally raised her hand to his. Pulling her up out of the chair, he led her to the small wooden dance floor in the middle of the area. He nuzzled into her and gently whispered into her ear. "This is nice."

"Yes, it is," Domenica admitted. In return, she burrowed into his warmth, and more importantly, his strength. Something she needed at this moment in her life.

While they danced Ramon placed their main entrees at their seats giving another wink to Kade. He cleared their salad plates and returned to the elevator.

The couple continued to dance to the soft, soothing music that saturated every crevice of the romantic setting. Kade held her close to him wishing she wasn't part of his assignment. He could see himself settling down with someone like Domenica. He grasped her chin and lifted her head up, placing a gentle kiss on those scrumptious full lips. He realized it would take longer than a few dates to bed her, but he would win. That was a given. He always won.

Lima Bean, you really fucked her up good. Something else I'll have to fix for you. But oh, will I enjoy fixing it.

Chapter 11

A few more weeks had passed with quite a few more interesting dates with Kade. The man really knew how to impress and was always the gentleman. Not that she was into money, but each date demonstrated his wealth and the things it bought. Things all commonplace to Kade—like everyone could sit behind home plate at the Braves baseball game, like everyone could call at the last minute and get in to dine at Raphaella's five-star restaurant in downtown Atlanta, like every could arrange to be at Chris Hemsworth's movie premiere, *Thor: Love and Thunder*, with its first night right here in Atlanta and almost all of the cast in attendance. He never asked what something might cost. If he wanted it, he bought it for her or brought her to it. She was happy he stopped pressuring her about her former relationships and seemed to enjoy being in her company. She certainly was enjoying him.

She thought of him as she entered the front door of The Library Bar and Grille and headed toward the bar. She was in early to prepare her area for her evening shift. Hopefully, tips would fly into her cup tonight.

She daunted tight black leather pants with stiletto boots, a red bustier trimmed in black lace and a ruby pendant that hung into her cleavage. Actually, if the ruby stone on her necklace had been a piece of coal, by the end of the night it would have turned into a diamond! That was how much pressure her cleavage pressed into it! The girls were up and pushed together tonight! It definitely drew the eye down to where she wanted the males to glare.

"Wow! Somebody is short on money this week," Nikki smirked as she approached to give Domenica the once-over. Nikki Freed was Domenica's roommate. There were many times the two fought like cats and dogs, especially when Domenica caught Nikki with her first love interest at the university, Dante Ciccone. But when Matt became the love of her life, it really didn't matter anymore.

"Last week was bad, so I'm taking your cue and dressing slutty to make up for my losses. You want our rent paid, don't you?"

"Since you've been dancing, I've noticed a lot more *daring* added to your wardrobe. And yes, I want the rent paid. My ass can't sleep on an outside bench." Nikki plunked her butt in its usual spot at the bar. "Do you think he will show up here tonight?" She turned to a server, "Can I have a piece of chocolate molten cake please?"

"Who will be here tonight?" Damon Burke asked as he walked by Domenica. The owner, John Michaels, hired Damon as a solo pianist to entertain the clientele until the place filled. That's when the dance music started.

"God, Nikki. Why don't you just go ask Damon to use the mic, so you can tell everyone in here?" She placed her glasses out and started to put her bottles in the order she preferred. "A guy I met might show up tonight, Damon, so Nikki came early to get a good seat to check him out."

"Maybe money wasn't the only reason you wore the leather and lace," Nikki quipped.

A few seconds later, the server plopped down the steaming cake on the bar in front of Nikki. As the dish rattled to stillness, Nikki lustfully gazed at it. "Damn, nothing like chocolate cake or an orgasm. It doesn't get better than that. In fact, many times, the cake is the better choice."

"Jesus, Nikki. Your mouth. By the way, I'll have you know I'm just keepin' it interesting."

"So you didn't do the nasty with him yet?"

"Um, my name is Domenica, not Nikki. We've only been going out for a few weeks, and I don't like him like that yet. Maybe not ever like that."

"What's *like* got to do with it? You said he was hot."

Domenica gave Damon a looked before she addressed Nikki. "I don't sleep with everyone I go out with, and I don't know if I'm over Matt yet."

"God, you are such a nerd and a dumb ass." Besides Domenica's roommate, Nikki was a swimmer on the CSU team. She also believed in having a lot of fun during her college days. She had always planned to sow a lot of oats and corn and peas and wheat! Whatever grain was out there! "I'm not over Matt," she repeated in a whiney voice, sarcastically ridiculing Domenica. "He broke up with you in a letter, he hasn't called, you don't know if he is coming back, geez Domenica. Wake up and get on this planet. He could have died, for all you know!"

"Nikki!" Damon chastised.

Domenica turned to Nikki somberly. "I loved him, Nikki. Still do. Sure, he wasn't this muscle-bound superstar. He wasn't rich. He wasn't even settled in his life yet." She paused, thinking about how Matt thought he was doing the right thing for his country and humanity. "He was a quiet and gentle man who looked at me as though I was everything he needed to exist. My only prayer was that he'd always look at me like that. I loved him. But you wouldn't know anything about love, would you, Nikki?"

There was a long silence.

"I'm sorry, Domenica. I was just trying to motivate you to get back out there. Just trying to point out reality. Remember, I was the one who found you after your breakdown. It wasn't good. Remember? I'm sorry."

"Let's just talk about something else. I'm not mad, Nikki. I just need more time to 'get back out there.' At least I'm trying."

She felt like that little dandelion struggling to grow between two slabs of cement, all because the wind fatefully blew its seed there to germinate. Many had to struggle against what fate dished out, only to hope they could survive even in the worst circumstances.

She continued to set up her area, going into the kitchen to stack more clean glasses. She thought, *Get back out there. That is no easy endeavor.*

She started to think about Matt, how sometimes in the quiet of her day, she would just say his name.

"Matt."

To help her get through the times when she was alone, reflecting on her life's events, wondering what she could have done differently.

"Matt."

She would form his name on her lips and slowly push the air through, so it would linger longer, so she could feel the humming sound of it vibrating on her lips, as if he were kissing her. Once past her lips, the sound would curl around her ears.

"Matt."

Sometimes when she was around others, she would whisper it softly as though it were this great universal prayer chanted to ease the souls of the desolate. It did, it gave her solace, and it gave her peace, just saying his name in the quiet of the day. Even through all these months later—even dating Kade—sometimes she would just say his name to remember what magical love felt like.

As she returned to the bar, she noticed Nikki was all over someone, laughing and flirting. She knew who it was just by the reaction of every other female in the room staring with envious eyes.

Kade Abraham.

When she saw him, she thought about how he could have been Lucifer's poster boy for erotic temptation, the deep darkened immoral actions women confessed of either doing or dreamed about doing in the blackness of the confessional booth to their stunned priest—the man who'd heard every type of sin ever committed! Priests had to have given them thousands of Hail Mary's to say and a few full rosaries to recite for their sin-of-Kade penance.

He had this potent presence when he walked through a room, oozing an omnipotent power that seethed out of him and descended over every other life form.

Christ, she thought, *Maybe he is Lucifer!*

Suddenly, he saw her. With his eyes, he could touch her as they slid down her body memorizing her every curve.

My God! If he could do that with his eyes, what could he do with the rest of his body parts? Maybe one day I will find out. When I am sure there is no more Matt.

"Domenica!" He pushed past Nikki, rushed to her, took her hand, and kissed it as though he were the prince who had just awakened her from the long nightmare. He certainly made her smile.

"I see you met my roommate." She gave a death-stare to Nikki, who had quickly backed off Kade when Domenica emerged from the back room.

"Yes, Nikki and Damon have given me a lot of useful information about you." He glanced back at her grinning, while *her* glance toward Nikki and Damon was more of the poisonous-arrow-coming-at-you type. "Can I sit here for the evening?" He drew her attention back to him.

"Yes. You will be out of the way sitting there." She turned around quickly under the pretense of filling an order, but the real reason was that he just sat where Matt used to sit. Domenica didn't know if she should go out with him anymore. Only that it was not fair to him. Yes, she really liked him, but her feelings for Matt got in the way—every damn time she was with him.

He reached over the bar pulling her to him and whispered into her ear. "Damn, you look, you look like, you look… Excuse me for this but… God, I want to fuck you right now, right here in that slutty outfit! My tongue all over your tits."

She still could not get over how he just blatantly said what he felt. Blatantly!

She turned to see the lust in his eyes. "Well, I was going for the sophisticated-sexy look, but apparently I achieved that I-look-so-slutty-that-men-come-up-to-me-and say to-me-I-want-to-fuck-you look." She gave him a devious smile, as he threw his head back in that loud masculine laughter of his.

"Well!" He still had that lascivious smile on his face. "I think you failed with the sophisticated-sexy look, but I am *not* complaining." His eyes continued to take her in as he ordered a drink. "Can you get me a scotch on the rocks, my beauty?"

She started making his drink as Nikki leaned over the bar and whispered in her ear. "And now you have to choose between a New York Strip and a filet mignon? Oh yeah, your life is just *soooo* tough."

Domenica ignored her, finished pouring, and then placed the drink in front of Kade. He was staring at her, giving her the once-over again specifically stopping his *eyejourn* on her chest —that was the new word she'd made up from the word sojourn completely appropriate for how men blatantly stared down a woman's body.

She truly appreciated Kade's attentiveness of her, but Matt had her trapped in this limbo. Would he return to her, would he not? How could she go on with her life if she perpetually floated in this void between Heaven and Hell?

She did not have to see Matt to feel him around her, on her, in her. Did she even want to dispel his memory? It was the flotation device around her, protecting her from drowning in sorrow. Therefore, her definitive conflict: Matt, who was not here and might never be here, or Kade, who was.

"Are you busy this weekend?" Kade wished she would open up to him. She was a tough safe to crack. Matt apparently did a number on her, and every man after him would suffer for it. She and he enjoyed each other's company on their dating endeavors. He enjoyed her a little too much.

She still stayed guarded even though she allowed him to obtain some yardage with her body a few times. She just would not let him score in the end zone. Very frustrating indeed.

He never had to try this hard before. He knew women were attracted to him, even threw themselves at him. He went through women like he used to go through video games when he was a kid. Once he solved the game, on to the next, newest challenge.

He remembered the Colonel's comment, "I'm paying you extra not to be entrapped in her enticing web." He was trying. He really was trying. Insects know not to fly close to that beautiful web, but it draws them in. He shouldn't sleep with her, but he knew he had to and when he did, would he be strong enough to pull away?

"Kade? Kade? What about this weekend? I said I was free Saturday."

"Oh! I, um," He jerked back to the present. "I wanted to take you to my favorite restaurant." *In Tuscany, in Italy,* he thought. *It's time to pull out the biggest guns.* "How about Sunday and Monday too."

Shannon, eavesdropping as she approached the bar, answered for Domenica. "She will go to dinner with you. I know for a fact she has nothing planned."

"Shannon!" Domenica turned to Kade. "I would be delighted to go. Just so we both understand that it's only dinner as friends. Nothing more."

"Why Domenica! You insult me. I am only thinking of spending quality time with you. I'm also thinking of eating for some reason." Once again, the lascivious smile.

"That's what I'm afraid of." She certainly had her hands full with this one.

Chapter 12

"Remind me again why I have to pack a small suitcase to go to dinner?" Domenica stood in the kitchen finishing the evening dishes wondering why Nikki and Shannon were acting so strange.

"Inclement weather? What if you spill something on you? Are you going to walk around with a stain all day? Kade said it was a few hours away." Nikki asserted.

"What if your stomach bloats? Didn't your mom teach you to always be prepared?" Shannon was trying to remain steady, but Kade had told her the plan to fly Domenica to Tuscany. He had to make sure she had a current passport.

Strange couldn't even come close to the two girls' behavior tonight.

Shannon had to sneak Domenica's passport into a compartment of the overnight bag and then there were the extra clothes. Nikki had to keep her busy so Shannon could finish her designated task.

"And are you really going to go around all day without refreshing your makeup?" Nikki yelled out.

Earlier Shannon and she ran around clandestinely collecting toiletries and makeup slipping them in under the few changes of clothing and a nightie.

Before that, she even slipped in Domenica's sexiest underwear and a few packs of her own condoms—just in case. Hmm. She would be sure to count them on Domenica's return.

Shannon and Nikki went for a high-five when their job was completed. All the giggling girls had to do now was sneak the bag into Kade's car when he arrived a few hours from now, just so Domenica would not be able to go through it. They even planned a fake excursion with Domenica for the evening so she would be ready to leave with Kade tonight.

"Okay. Dishes are done. I'm going to get ready. Are we still wearing jeans?" Domenica started for her room.

"Yes, but dress sexy cuz you know that's how we roll."

Within an hour, Domenica entered the kitchen walking as though she were America's highest paid model. "Dawling, dawling." She strutted her stuff. "Now you both need to rise to my level." She donned her favorite show-off-my-ass jeans with a royal blue clingy jersey top. The cowl neckline would open to display her matching lace cami if she stooped too low. Shannon and Nikki just looked at each other with approving smiles on their faces.

"Now that's how it's done," Nikki proclaimed thinking her gift of condoms might get some use after all. Domenica went in search of her handbag when the doorbell rang out.

"Who could that be?" Shannon tried not to be obvious.

"I'll get it." Domenica reached for the doorknob and pulled it open. "Kade?"

"It looks like you are ready to go."

"Our dinner date is tomorrow." Domenica replied in confusion.

"Yes. The date is indeed tomorrow, but we need to travel tonight to get to my favorite restaurant." Kade had that debonair look on his face.

"Travel tonight? Where?"

"You are going to Tuscany, Italy," Shannon blurted out, grabbing Domenica and almost jumping on her in excitement.

Stunned, Domenica scrutinized first Nikki's, then Shannon's, then Kade's face. Two held excitement and joy, Kade's had a meek grin. "I wanted to surprise you, so the ladies helped me out."

Shannon started first. "We thought that—"

"Shannon, Nikki. Out. Now." Domenica's voice boomed.

"But—"

"Out! Go to your rooms!"

"Um, my room is upstai—"

"Go!"

Heads hanging, both girls trudged to Nikki's room slamming the door shut.

"Domenica, I thought—"

"Stop right there. Kade." She almost pushed her flat hand into his face. She calmed down a second and continued, "I told you I could not promise you anything. I told you we would take this slow. How could you do this to me?"

"Domenica, it's just a jaunt to Italy. I have a private plane and pilot. I just wanted to take you somewhere nice. That's all. Maybe somewhere so you would never forget me." He stated the last remark in a dejected tone, pretty much putting every card from his playbook on the table.

"And when we stop going out will I hear how I took you for all you had, how I played you, how you were just the person I used to get through my sadness?

No. I can't do that to you, Kade. I won't do that to you. I have started to care for you. I love you, Kade."

"Domenica!" Kade started toward her with a look of joy on his face.

She stopped him. "But not in the way you want me to love you. I won't hurt you because *ti amo*, Kade."

"Ti amo?" Kade repeated quizzically.

"It means I love you in Italian, and I do. Just not the way you want."

"Domenica, please. I won't say any of that. I'm not the young man you fell for, the one who hurt you. I'm an adult who knows sometimes relationships last, and sometimes they don't. Yes, I do love you and yes, to be honest, I wish you were in my bed every night. The thoughts I have about you are erotically sinful!" His smile deepened as his eyes softened their stare. "But, it's not just that. *You* make me laugh. *You* make me feel good about myself. *You* make me realize that I could have a lot more, could be a lot more—with you or not. I never thought I would want a relationship with a woman. But if I found you, and we don't work out, I now know there's a chance that there could be another one. That I could have these feelings and share my life with someone. Domenica, *ti amo*."

"Kade, I—"

"Let me finish. Your Matt was a fool." He walked back and forth, while he brushed his hand through his hair. "I don't know the circumstances because you don't trust me enough to open up, even though I asked you to share your sadness with me. All I ask is give me a chance. I might never have your love the way I want it, but God, I want the chance to try to earn it. Domenica, I would give up the whole damn farm for you!"

There was a long, long silence as they stared at each other. Slowly, she smiled at him. "Including the back forty acres?"

"It's more like a four thousand square foot penthouse in Florida, but yes." He returned her smile.

She flew to his arms crashing into him sobbing. Kade placed his chin on her head and held on as if she were his life jacket. "Domenica, however long it takes. However long. *Ti amo*, Domenica"

"I'm just so lost, Kade. I still have feelings for him, but you just tsumanied yourself into my life, so I have these feelings for you too."

"Tsunamied? Is that a word?"

"Well, if Shakespeare can make up words, so can I." She snuggled closer into him controlling her tears.

"Hey, we will figure this out together. Okay?"

She shook her head, separated from him, and wiped her eyes. "No regrets?" She needed assurance.

"No." Kade quickly answered.

"No unspoken promises?"

"No."

"No expectations?"

Kade was slow to answer this one. "Well, um. There is always hope. You know I'm the kind of man who must reach for the gold. But I did book two rooms." That was a lie, but he smiled at her as he used his thumb to wipe a tear slowly glazing her cheek. "Come with me. Step out of your turmoil and just live a little this weekend. Just let yourself feel peace."

She thought a moment.

"Okay." She said it as though she were facing a firing squad that was aimed at her. "I'll have to go and pack."

"No you don't." Shannon rushed from the back room. "Oops." Apparently, the girls were listening. "I mean… Nikki and I already packed a bag for you. All you really have to do is add any other clothes to it."

Kade interrupted. "Listen, I'll be back in an hour. Go through your bag. Be ready to go. I'll make some time changes for the flight." He kissed her goodbye and went out their door.

As he slid into his car, he buckled up and punched the steering wheel with both hands. He slammed down on it again. "Fuck, fuck, and fuck!" he screamed out. He thought about everything he said to her and realized it was easy for him to say all of that to her because it wasn't a lie at all. It was all true. He was falling and falling fast. Everything was true except for the part that they might not work out.

If Matt came back, that would be the wrench in his plan. Of course, when he killed Matt, he would have no competition. Problem solved, and Domenica would never know.

Chapter 13

Kade buckled her in next to him as his jet prepared for departure. Suddenly, as he slipped in past her, his pen fell from his jacket to the floor. Domenica instinctively bent down to pick it up. When he turned to sit down, his passport clumsily fell to the floor. Again, Domenica bent down, but this time she stopped and slowly turned her head to see Kade copping a view down her top."

"You are incorrigible, Kade Abraham," Domenica exclaimed as she slapped his arm.

"What? I told you the views from a plane were spectacular." He waggled his brows confidently.

"I assumed you meant the views of Earth from the air."

"Yes, well, that too." He leaned over and placed a gentle kiss on her cheek. He interpreted that her meek smile was a sign to continue, so he nibbled on her ear and started to kiss down her neck. His breath grew rapid and his dick reciprocated, growing semi-hard. What this woman could fucking do to him in a second!

"Kade." She shifted away from him, a difficult task—to push away from this force of nature. He was unique in that she could not compare him to anyone she had even known. He carried this masculine energy with him. His presence, his attitude, his masculine smell, his physique. She wanted to be in his arms. She wanted to forget about everything else. "Kade, please." She had to fight the connection.

"I love when you beg," he whispered hoarsely in her ear.

"That's not what I'm doing." Her irritated voice snarled.

Kade took the not-so-subtle hint and shifted to sit straight up in his seat. "I know. I know! Fuck!" He yelled, dragging his hand through his hair. "Domenica, I can't help wanting to touch you, to kiss you. Damn, even to hold you." He yelled to the flight attendant, "Can you bring me a scotch on the rocks please. Make it a double." He addressed Domenica. "You want anything?"

"I'll take the same," she answered adamantly.

"What? You need a strong drink to deal with me?"

"Leave it alone, Kade."

Then, he adjusted his hard dick and mumbled just loud enough for her to hear, "Fuck! This is going to be a long flight."

The flight attendant brought their drinks. "Sir, ma'am, if you want anything else, I'll be up front. Just push the call button. I have pillows and blankets over here. I assume that you will be sleeping sometime between the twelve-hour flight. Once again, if you need anything."

Domenica noticed she addressed the last few words to Kade with a seductive countenance. *The dumb bitch! Does she not think I might be his girlfriend?*

Domenica turned her gaze out the window as the aircraft skirted down the runway and ascended into the vast sky. She did not even realize she captured Kade's arm and was squeezing the life out of it.

Kade studied her as she returned his stare and slowly released his arm. A thought occurred to him. *Yep, I would give up the whole damn farm for her including the back forty. Ti amo, Domenica.*

***

"Domenica. Domenica!" Kade's sexy, deep voice reverberated as he gently shook her.

Like a garage door commanded by a remote, Domenica's eyelids slowly lifted to see, first, sky blue gemstones of shiny topaz surrounded by the blackest, long lashes. Next, dark eyebrows arched together in a quizzical countenance over those jeweled eyes. As she opened her lids wider, the straight-lined, aristocratic nose materialized followed by sensuously thick, kissable lips. Finally, with eyes wide open, a dark shadowed chin and cheeks in a Grecian-shaped face appeared, all capped with glossy black, disheveled hair that hands could get lost in while making love. A smiling face. A strong face. Sadly for her, an adoring face. Kade.

She quickly sat up still staring into his eyes. His eyes, glued to hers, seemed to be searching for the portal leading into her soul, the portal she now kept closed. He leaned down and gently pressed his lips to her forehead.

"Good morning, angel. We'll be landing at the Pisa International Airport in Pisa in a few."

Yawning, Domenica finally broke contact and stretched. "Mmmmmmm. Wait! We're here? How long was I asleep? What time is it?"

"9:00 a.m. our time, 3:00 p.m. their time. Are you ready to dine with me for breakfast? At 3:00 p.m.?" He smiled squeezing her hand. She noticed he always found a way to touch her somehow, to make a connection. She didn't want to love that he did that, but she did. As she gazed into his face, she wondered what might have been if she'd met him before Matt.

Her moral standards were now arguing with her. Everyone she knew told her to forget Matt. But how fickle would she be? She had proclaimed this great love for him, fell to pieces when he left, now only to fall for another man a few months later? She would not be that faithless and fickle woman.

There was definitely a sexual connection with Kade, a dangerous, sexual connection with Kade. Just look at him. Any woman who laid eyes on him stared in appreciation of the day God chose to show off His creative artistry. Kade was sculpted masculinity to within a degree of perfection. A dominant personality promising safety and love and alpha sexuality.

After the smooth landing, both took turns using the small bathroom and then started to exit the aircraft. He led her down the steps to the waiting car. When they were comfortable in the back seat, Kade called out their destination to the driver. "I thought we would drive through the Chianti region between Florence and Sienna." As he placed his hand over hers, he quipped, "I don't know about you, but I'm starving. Can we stop at a café to *mangia?*"

"*Sì. Voglio mangiare qualcosa.* And since that is wine country, we might partake in some vino too."

Kade's look was sheer amazement. "You speak Italian?"

"*Parlo un po.*" She held her index finger and thumb about an inch apart. "I'm better at listening to it or reading it to understand, but I can get by. My problem is I mix Spanish with Italian."

"Well, hell. You are going to be my interpreter."

"Oh, and how much will I get paid for this service, sir?"

"Um. We *could* take it out in trade, maybe? I was told I'm amaaaazing!" Kade's devilish eyes beamed at her again. "Just a thought."

"Your problem is *that* seems to be your only thought!" She returned his smile, as Kade instructed the driver to stop at the next small café or restaurant.

The drive was a delight to the senses. Just as in the pictures of Italy, the countryside was strewn with fields of vineyards and lush silver hues of olive groves, all drizzled by the warm golden rays of the sun. They traveled on winding country roads lined with tall, green cypress trees. These giants also accented the borders of large patches of fields. Either Domenica pointed something out for Kade to see, or he pointed something else out for her to see. Both were in awe of the tranquil beauty surrounding them.

Domenica remarked, "It feels like God dropped us into an oil painting."

She smiled at Kade. He enjoyed how she delighted in every minute of the drive. He suddenly realized he was deriving this joy from her joy. That never, ever happened before in his life. He was the first to admit that he was a selfish man, but today and the last few weeks that he had known Domenica, he realized his happiness was born out of hers.

Chapter 14

The small villages they passed seemed right out of the medieval era, many of the homes built of stone. Suddenly, the driver turned into a tourist guide. "Dis isa da so-calt Chianti Triangela. Eetsa how you say three townza together. Many restortantes and much wine tasting. We stoppa in Castellina." Kade and Domenica agreed.

Soon, they excited the car and soon were seated in a secluded area in what looked like a restored farm building made of stone. It had a clay-tiled roof. Located on the outskirts of the city, the building had massive beams made from tree trunks holding up the wooden-planked ceiling. Beautiful.

A server approached them. "*Vuole iniziare ad ordinare da bere?*"

Domenica turned to Kade. "He wants to know what you would like a drink."

"Chianti Rosato." Kade replied as he perused the wine list.

"*Due, per favore.*" Domenica reiterated the order. The server bowed to them as he left to fill the drink order. "Kade?"

"Yes?" Kade was now scrutinizing the interior.

"Thank you."

"What?" He edged toward her. "For what?" He was not sure where this was going.

"For everything. I mean, I know you tend to be the alpha dog. That's your nature. But, with me, you tend to pull that personality in a bit. I just wanted you to know that I appreciate that and all of this. For a few days, I know I will experience peace of mind. You did that for me, and I will never forget it." She softly smiled at him as she grabbed and squeezed his hand. "Ti amo, Kade." Releasing his hand, she opened the menu to examine it.

For once in his life, Kade had no idea what to say. He felt guilty as fuck. More than fuck. Here he was, scoping her out so she would disclose Matt's whereabouts for the sole purpose of killing him. Besides that, he brought her to Italy to impress and seduce her. He really was a fucking dickwad.

He never really met anyone like Domenica. Most of the women he met and associated with were more than likely *under* the bar stools at those dive bars he frequented when hunting. Of course, he always just wanted an easy lay, so the drunker they were, the better. Drunk and willing. But Domenica? She still believed in people. She saw the good that no one else saw. She believed in love, even after whatever Matt did to her. Yes, Matt was a fucking dickwad too.

The server placed their wine in front of them. *"Ha già deciso?"*

"Do you want me to order for you, Kade?"

"Yes, a steak please."

She began, *"Signore, prego. Risotto Carnaroli mantecato al pecorino di fossa, and la costata per due persone servita con verdure grigliate."*

"Vuole l'antipasto?"

"Do you want an antipasto, Kade? We ordered rice, steak for two, grilled vegetables and of course vino."

Kade stretched in his chair. "Naw. I think that is more than enough."

"No antipasto. *Grazie*." The server took the menus as Domenica again studied the interior of the restaurant.

She thought about how her mother had found a four-leaf clover while she was walking in their yard. She picked it and pressed it between the pages of a hardbound book to preserve it. She now understood that her mom probably did that gesture to be able to re-visit a moment of awe in her life, the day when she found something rare and beautiful. Domenica wanted to press this time, these moments of awe, this memory with Kade between the folds of her brain, so she could reopen them back up when she needed to re-visit a moment of serenity and joy.

***

Kade sipped his wine admiring her. He too reflected on a memory, one that also slowly crept into his mind. He was a child. His mother brought him to a museum presenting the works of a famous artist. *Who was that person again?* No, he could not remember the man's name. He did remember the beauty of the paintings.

He walked up to one and started to reach for it when his mother yelled out, *"Kade!"* She quickly grabbed his arm, pulling him back, and stooped to his level. "You are not allowed to touch that. Stand back," she said to him. "Sometimes we don't mean to destroy something so beautiful but accidents happen. At your age, I just can't trust you near the paintings. So you are to stay away from the pieces. We shall admire beauty from afar." With his mother holding his hand, the two of them stood back as far as they could, perusing and appreciating the works of art.

That's how he *should* be with Domenica. He should be admiring her from afar, not escorting her to Italy. However, once he saw that beauty, inside and out, he just could not stay away. He had to touch it. His mother was right. This close, accidentally or not, he could destroy her. How did these feelings materialize? He had to gain control over them no matter what.

"Listen to the background song," Domenica said. "My *nonna* used to sing this to us. 'O Sole Mio.'" Her eyes filled with tears. "I haven't heard that song in a long time. It's amazing how that song triggered so many memories of my nonna. I used to love helping her roll her meatballs." Domenica froze, eyes wide open again. "And no comment from you about making meatballs."

Kade's robust laugher filled the room so loudly that other clients turned to stare at him. "Well, I certainly did not expect you to enjoy something like that, although I do have some meatballs you can roll. That is, if you are feeling nostalgic." He whispered the last remark close to her ear—anything to be close to her skin.

Now, it was her turn to laugh. "I knew you would make a comment as soon as I said that. I just knew it."

Kade stood and reached out his hand to her. "May I have this dance?"

"But there's no one else—"

He pulled her up and drew her into him. Domenica placed her head on his massive chest and for the first time in a long time, peace cascaded over her. Something else to press into the folds of her brain. They spent the next few hours dancing, eating, and drinking Italian wine.

Domenica giggled as she finished her fourth glass of Chianti. "I am going to become a millionaire and buy a villa here in Tuscany."

As he reached for her hand, he declared seriously, "Marry me, and you can have two." She sadly smiled at him. He rose from his seat and helped her up.

Domenica stumbled a little, giggling again, "Silly. I can't marry you. That would ruin our friendship status."

"Oh, but it would certainly help in our physical status." Kade drew her close to him, her lips just a whisper away from his. He looked into her eyes wishing he could read her thoughts. If he could only get her to physically act on their connection.

"Kade, please don't." she pleaded in his ear.

A few seconds of stillness lapsed, then he kissed her forehead and said, "Come on, I have something to show you." He paid the bill and led her back to the car, his arm around her waist to aid in her tipsy walking. They drove a few miles toward their hotel when all of a sudden he had the driver stop the car.

"We are getting out here."

***

On both sides of the road were acres of beautiful vineyards with rows and rows of vines tied to the trellis wires. He led her into one of the massive vineyards.

Just as Italian food was a feast for the stomach, the vineyards were feasts for the eyes. Colorful hues of muted olive green on flat lands or rolling hills, yellowish-green grapes variegated to deep shades of purple floating on bright green leaves all clinging to reddish vines, and azure blue skies with the largest yellow sun shining down on all of it. The vineyards looked like rows of astute soldiers in formation for morning stationary drills of attention. As the two of them walked in deeper and deeper, she held his hand persistently.

"Come on, let's run," she yelled out to him. "It smells so wonderful. I feel like I'm in a jar of grape jelly." She let go of his hand and started to twirl, laughing throughout.

"At least you're a happy drunk." Kade watched her in delight, but ran to her when she started to stumble. "Domenica, I don't think you should—"

Too late. Kade went to grab her, but she toppled over with him tumbling down on top of her.

"Domenica!"

She looked up into his face and started laughing in a boisterous sound; the sound infiltrating the rows of grapevines around them.

"I guess you're didn't get hurt." He laughed along with her.

All at once, their surroundings transformed. As her laughter faded, she looked at his face, deep into those penetrating eyes. Ever so slowly, his lips sunk toward hers. Slowly. Slowly. The movement—snaillike. Kade's lips touched hers delicately, fearing she would recoil. Amazingly, she returned the kiss instead.

With his arms straddled on each side of her, he kissed each corner of her mouth, then the tip of her nose. She giggled looking up at him. He smiled into her laughter. He returned to her mouth and quietly glided his tongue across her top lip then bottom lip, and she reciprocated with her tongue gently touching his.

With that one gesture on her part, his breathing quickened. His tongue penetrated her mouth and exploded inside, attacking hers. The battle began. She retaliated to the attack, kissing back brazenly.

"Domenica," Kade whispered. "I fucking want you so bad. I need you to be mine." His hands gently roamed her body; he took both her arms and placed them above her head. He knew he was about to enter Nirvana. "God, Domenica, I want to fill that pussy of yours, I want to live in you." he whispered again. "Ti amo. Let me fuck you. Let me make love to you. Please." He was begging. Kade never begged.

She pulled her arms loose and wrapped them around his neck, quickly maneuvering one hand into his thick hair where she dug her fingers, grabbing and pulling. She could hear his elevated breath gasping for air between kisses, his clothes swishing against hers, his powerful heartbeat drumming in his chest. His powerful chest mashing against her breasts.

His hands wandered down her body needing to feel every inch of her, trying to explore something that she might just lend to him for only a moment in time. Her waist, her curved hips, her heavy breasts. The kissing became unrestricted. She bit his lower lip. He sucked on her lips. They could not seem to satiate their desire. His hand went to her clit rubbing it through her clothes. "Domenica," he called out. He gasped for air as she broke away from the kiss to gently whisper a name into his ear too.

"Matt."

Silence.

All movement stopped.

Acutely.

Abruptly.

Silence.

"Kade?"

Silence.

"Kade. Please. I didn't mean to… Say something."

Silence.

It was that eerie silence; the kind that followed a tornado after it wiped out everything. That stillness in a thick air where the quiet was powerful.

Chapter 15

"I'm sor—"

Kade pushed up from her and expeditiously walked back toward the car.

"Kade, please. I'm sorry. Seriously. I didn't mean to call you Matt. I—"

Domenica abruptly stood up to chase after him, but only made it a few steps before she grabbed a vine to hold on to while she vomited up the wine, the food, and, symbolically, Kade's dream.

Kade stopped just for a moment. He had to help her. *Christ, I love her. Oh my God! I. Love. Her. For sure! No maybes. Not I might love her. I do love her!*

How fucking stupid was he? He rushed to her side quickly lifting her hair. She vomited until she had nothing left in her stomach. Kade reached into his pocket and handed her his handkerchief.

As she wiped her mouth, she started crying. Deep heavy sobs. Into his shirt. "Kade. Please forgive me. Please, Kade." She hiccupped throughout her pleas. "Kade, I—"

"Shh. Come on, we are not going to ruin our vacation over a slip of the tongue. Okay?"

She looked into his tender eyes. "Okay. Forgive me, Kade. Please," she hiccupped repeatedly. "Please forgive me, Kade."

Kade knew it was more than a slip of the tongue, but he also knew baby steps. He nodded to her and held her close guiding her back to the car.

***

In the hotel room, Kade helped her out of the I-stink-so-bad-of-vomit clothes and wiped her down with a warm washcloth. Then, he helped her into one of his t-shirts, placed her into bed turning her on her side toward his temporary garbage-can-puke-bucket, and covered her just to her waist. It turned out she was *not* a happy drunk; she had crying jags all the way to the hotel and even as he helped her change for bed. He sat watching her, content that he was just spending this time with her, just the two of them—even though she was pretty much comatose.

He never realized that love was also about cleaning up someone's puke. They never showed that in a movie! Yet, here he was, standing guard over her and loving every minute of it.

How fucking stupid was he? He was a logical man, very left-brain, but he now found something that defied even logic. It was love.

His job was to complete a contract on a man she loved deeply. If he did this, and she ever found out, she would despise him forever. If he did not complete this, the Colonel would probably have a contract out on him. Fuck!

Domenica sighed in her sleep as he continued to stare at her well into the early hours of the morning. Later, he would figure this out. Right now, he had to get some sleep. He stripped down to his boxers, adjusted the puke bucket where he could easily push her toward it if need be, and crawled into bed cuddling next to a woman who would probably unknowingly destroy him. Love certainly threw logic right out the window. Although touching her this close, he didn't even give a shit. How was that for fucking logic?

***

A few hours later when the sun peeked over the rolling hills, apparently awakened by the same boisterous rooster that called to Domenica, she felt a pressure over her rib cage and intense heat in the back of her neck. She rolled to her back and, as she slowly turned her head more, she almost grazed Kade's nose with her own. He was in a deep sleep, his chest rising and falling rhythmically. Her face jerked back to the ceiling.

What the fuck? Think, Domenica, think! She tried to remember the events of their late afternoon dinner together. *Wine, food, more wine, more food, music, more wine, more food, dancing, more wine. Oh God!*

She remembered him helping her to the car. After that, everything else was a pool of muddy water. *Wait! Walking through the vineyards, kissing, him laying on top of me, kissing, touching, grabbing, him calling out my name, me calling out... Oh God! I said Matt. I. Fucking. Said. Matt.*

Lifting the comforter over her, she slipped quietly out of bed, almost hitting the wastebasket that Kade apparently placed there. She stealthily tiptoed to the bathroom. There hanging over the vanity were her clothes drying.

Okay, now I remember vomiting. Poor Kade! I have to shower; I smell like vomit. After she turned on the shower, she lifted off her t-shirt... *Wait. This is Kade's shirt.*

What the fuck. She realized that she had nothing on under his t-shirt. *Oh no. Did we… I mean, could he have…*

She quickly jumped under the warm water still trying to remember what the hell happened after they returned to the hotel room. Throwing the hotel robe on, she walked into the bedroom to see Kade propped up against the pillows staring out the facing window in a reverie.

"How bad was it?" She meekly smiled at him.

"Oh, it was bad." He stared at her. "You called me Matt when we were making out. You pretty much cut off my balls *and* my dick! Not to mention parts of my ass cheeks and my prostate. In fact, anything at all remotely connected to my manhood is now gone! Do I still have a beard?"

Her head dropped. Then she looked up at him through teary lashes. "Then how did we—" If calling him Matt upset him this much, she could not imagine what not remembering their first sexual encounter would do to him. Trying a humorous approach, she turned red thinking how in the fuck to ask if they had sex.

"Oh, we didn't," he asserted, knowing where she was headed with this. "Look, Domenica, I am not a good man."

As she tried to disagree, he put his flat hand up stopping her. "Like I said, I am not a good man, but I would never, ever take advantage of any woman who wasn't willing and pretty much comatose. Just as I will *not* accept being a fill-in for a long lost love." With that, he hopped out of bed and headed to the bathroom.

"Kade." She grabbed his arm turning him to face her. "I didn't do that on purpose. I would never hurt you on purpose. You are the only one who has brought any type of happiness into my life these last few months." She fought back those clinging tears.

Kade pulled her close to him wrapping his arms around her, his cheek against her hair. "I know, Domenica, I know. I just need to realize that no matter how much you try to make someone love you the same as you love them, the plan doesn't always work. Maybe it never works."

Domenica pulled back and stared at him, astonished. *Love?*

"Yes, I love you, Domenica. I figured that out last night. And not an I-love-my-friend type of love. I mean the I-want-to-throw-you-down-on-that-mattress-and-press-you-into-it-as-I-thrusts-deep-into-you kind of love. I. Want. You. Domenica." He paused a moment. "No pressure. I am not going to kidnap you and force you to marry me." He chuckled as she smiled up at him. "I don't even know how or when it happened. I just know it did." He started to walk back to the bathroom, "Well, at least for me it did. The heart wants what it wants and all that fucking shit." With that, he slammed the bathroom door leaving Domenica stunned with his confession.

***

If anyone had told Kade he would be in Italy, on a Sunday morning, in a small church, at 8:00 a.m., attending mass, with a beautiful woman, humming along with the congregation's songs, in a language he did not understand, and enjoying it, he would have told that person to seek mental help or to go fuck off.

Nope, not Kade Abraham. He spent his Sunday mornings with his conquest of the prior evening, fucking her one more time before he pushed her out the door. However, church it was, with Domenica, for an hour, in the early morning, listening to a priest, about God knows what, and certainly not understanding a damn thing that was going on. Did he enjoy it? Every goddamn minute of it. He even remembered saying a silent prayer. *God, make me worthy of her.* Yeah, like God was going to listen to a killer.

As he contemplated their morning excursion, he sat placidly in the hotel room where room service just wheeled in their morning brunch. Domenica poured him a cup of coffee when Kade said to her, "I think I have a right to know."

"Know what?" Domenica looked like that little puppy that tilts its head and scrunches its brows in a mass of confusion.

"Know what happened with you and your Matt." Kade placed two plates at the little table in the room, directing her to sit.

There was a long silence. As she sat, she glanced down at her plate.

"I met him at the bar," she started, "an out-of-towner. There was instant chemistry." She thought about everything she would say next, as she stirred her coffee. "He told me he was a computer analyst, but he wasn't. He lied. We dated for a few months and kept it casual. He even went home with me over Christmas, met my family, and they all loved him too."

Now for the difficult part to tell. She looked up at him. "I took him to Cleveland's Rock and Roll Hall of Fame where someone shot at us."

"What? Jesus Christ!" Kade stopped eating and listened intensely.

As she twirled her fork in her food, she continued. "He reasoned that it was random like in other cities and talked me into not saying anything because my parents would be upset. You know, ruin Christmas." She looked again to watch Kade's reaction. "When we returned to Atlanta, he planned the perfect date. We, um, spent New Year's Eve and day together in this beautiful hotel. That's when it went from casual to an intimate relationship. He was the only one I've ever been with."

She continued studying Kade as she finished. "A few days later, he left me for good with only a note. In it, he explained everything. He worked for an OGA; he was one of their best operatives, a hired sniper for the OGA. He wanted to quit, but he said they threatened my family and me. He said by the people who hired him. Except after a week, he came back. They shot him instead."

"Why the hell did they shoot him?" Kade played innocent.

"Um, he first threatened to quit because they paid him to shoot someone he didn't want to. He said he didn't sign up for that."

"Wow."

"Anyway, Matt was pretty bad, so I put him in an empty room I knew of," she lied, "and had someone who owed me a favor stay with him and help me nurse him back to health." Again, she lied at this part of the story to protect Jamal and Dawan. "When he was good enough to travel, we said our goodbyes, and he left. He told me he might never be able to return, but if he could, he would. Soooo, I'm here in limbo." She tried to wipe away the tear sliding down her cheek. "More like hell itself."

Kade touched her other hand as she added, "Kade, I wasn't trying to play you. I truly care for you. But I just can't," She started to sob, "I just can't promise you anything." She broke down as Kade jumped from his chair pulling her up to hold her.

"Hey. Don't cry, Domenica." He hated when she cried. He grabbed her arms and slightly shook her so she would focus on him. "I understand, and I did not think for a moment that you were trying to play me."

He pulled her into him as he realized that with her confession to him, she just signed her own death certificate.

Chapter 16

It was a moderately calm flight flying back home. He held her close to him while she tried to sleep.

"Domenica?"

"What?"

"Promise me you will never tell anyone else your story."

"Why?"

"Because these people sound dangerous, and I believe they would kill you for what you told me. Promise me!"

"Okay, Kade, I promise." She studied him obtusely.

What the fuck did he get himself into? With the long overnight flight, Kade planned his next moves. The first thing had to be keeping Domenica safe. To do that he would have to move her into one of his apartments, since he now realized hers was probably bugged. There, weekly, he could do sweeps to find any devices. Right now, he would sleep in the safety of the clouds holding on to the only important thing in his life. He made a few phone calls to his maintenance supervisor and, as his heavy eyes closed, he realized his only hope was to wait for Matt.

Would Matt show up? Yes, because colorful, aromatic flowers always draw the bee. He had to put this flower on full display for all to see, drawing the bee to its demise.

Driving back to Atlanta after the smooth flight landed, Kade started his plan. "Domenica? Are you really sorry for calling me Matt?"

"Kade, please. That was the most embarrassing thing I ever did to anyone and not intentional at all!" She quickly turned to look out her window, her face still turning a bright red.

"Then will you do something for me?" She turned back to look at him sizing him up. "Not that! Unless—"

"Well, at least *some* things haven't changed," Domenica quipped laughingly.

"Promise me you will do this."

"If I can, yes, I promise."

"Good. I have a three-bedroom apartment that I want you, and whomever you want, to move in to." He studied her countenance.

"Kade, I can't afford to—"

"Yes, you can, with two other roommates. I'll feel safer if you are where I can get to you, if the need arises."

"But I—"

"You said you would do anything. You. Owe. Me." He put his hand over his heart. "Calling me someone else while I was giving my best performance was traumatic. I may never be able to get a hard-on again!"

She smiled at this and countered, "Shouldn't your hand be on your dick then?"

He laughed putting his head down and lifting his platinum blue eyes in puppy dog style. "Say yes."

"But—"

"Say. Yes."

"Yes." She leaned in and kissed his cheek. Immediately, she started calling Shannon and Nikki to see who wanted to move in with her, as the car stopped in front of a large building. "We're at your place?"

"I assumed you wanted to help with my penis therapy, so I had the driver stop at the apartment so you could see it. You'll have the apartment beneath mine. I'm still on the top floor, of course." He came around the car to help her out as he whispered to her, "I knew I would get you under me somehow."

Domenica just shook her head as they walked into a stately building in an impressive area not far from the college and downtown life. "I'm going to live here? Under you?" The doorman greeted a stunned Domenica.

"Yes you are." Kade said as he nodded to the burly doorman. "*Under* me." Again that devious smile flashed.

They went up the elevator to the apartment where he opened the door and ushered her in. It was at least twice the size of her apartment. The living area was open-concept about thirty feet by thirty feet with an L-shaped front room and a kitchen with an island. Three chairs were pushed under the one side for eating.

"I'll have my contractor put a dance bar up, in this area, along with the wall-to-wall mirrors. I figured you can use it for dance practice with plenty of room over on this other side for a couch and chairs and TV."

He moved her to the bedrooms. "The bedrooms are small, but you can put a double in for two people or even bunks to utilize the space. A lot of closet room."

Domenica stared at the walk-in closets. In almost an involuntary response, she started jumping up and down and squealing. Then, she jumped into Kade's arms leaping at him and throwing him off balance. "Oh my God, oh my God, oh my God, oh my God!"

"Whoa!" He quickly caught her and made sure they both didn't fall over.

"Can we move in today? I'm calling Shannon and Nikki right now. Can I play loud music? I'm telling Eric we won't need to try to find a place to practice. Maybe I'll go a blue color scheme or maybe a—"

"Hold Up!" Kade pushed her back, smiling at her enthusiasm. "Are you telling me I spent all that money for us to go to Italy when all I had to do was get you a big walk-in closet? That's what made you jump into my arms?"

She pulled back and slapped his arm. "Yep, you found the way to a woman's heart. A *big* closet!"

"Hmmmmp! At least I knew it had to be *something* big. Oh, and just for your information, I'm big in the other department too." His eyebrows danced up and down.

"Hmm, good to know. I think I did see that advertised on your business card. *Big in all areas.*"

"Smart ass." He finished showing her the place. "Also, over here, this pocket door slides into this wall opening for this smaller room in the living area. It's too small for a bedroom but maybe it could be an office or another larger pantry, since the kitchen already has one. You figure it out. I don't even know why this is here, two walls with six feet of space in between. It just seems weird. I would have added this space to one of the bedrooms."

Domenica smiled as she called both girls letting both of them know they were moving on up. Of course, each one squealed into the phone and apparently asked a thousand questions that Domenica happily answered.

Chapter 17

Kade went up to his room to return the call he received from Colonel Masters. *This fucking prick is becoming a pain in my ass,* he thought as he dialed. As the phone rang, he dragged his suitcase into his bedroom to unpack.

"You took her to fucking Italy?" was the first explosion spewing from the Colonel's mouth. Kade had to pull back from the receiver.

"I'm trying to get her to open up more. She still doesn't trust me."

"You're fucking lying, boy. I know a lie when I hear one. Maybe *you* should disappear too." Filled with rage, Colonel Masters' veins dangerously bulged out of his neck.

Kade, not a man who dealt with threats, radiated an intense body heat as he controlled his temper to convince the Colonel that he was finishing the contract. "Do not ever threaten me again—ever! I told you I would get the job done, and I will. He has not come around, and she seems to believe that it is over, that he won't be back." He hoped he sounded convincing. "However, to help put you at ease, I moved her into an apartment in my building that I have bugged. There will be twenty-four hour surveillance."

"So for surveillance, or because it's more convenient for you to fuck her? What's that pussy like anyway?"

"Don't know. And believe me, I've tried everything. Besides, that will be difficult with two other roommates in the apartment. I told you she now has trust issues." He wanted to add *you fucking dickhead.*

"You've got one week to find him and kill him. One week! Oh, and Kade? I never threaten anyone. If I say it, I do it. You better remember that." *Bang!* He slammed the receiver down.

Kade sat for a while. This was fucking messed up. He never weaseled out of a contract. He knew the repercussions that action could bring. He had to devise a plan to save him and Domenica, and he knew just who could help him. Matt—if the fucker ever showed up. Kade would kill him and be back in the Colonel's graces and eventually in Domenica's bed.

***

Domenica put the last touches in her bathroom. The new apartment made all of her old possessions feel new. She walked into her big living area and tweaked her couch and chairs. Nikki even bought a new area rug to add that brand new feel. She loved all the space in here. She even put her large armoire in front of the door of that wasted six-foot room. The room was about eight feet deep so the girls put a few boxes of all their stored items in there, holiday decorations and whatnot, with plenty of room left. However, old place or new place, some things never change. Her cell rang.

Hurdling over a chair and running even more steps, she grabbed it by the third ring. "Hello?"

"Hey, beautiful. Are you all settled in yet?"

"Kade." He noticed lately that her voice softened when she said his name. That was a great sign. "I'm just rearranging things. You know how women are. It's gotta be perfect." She glanced over her work. "Thanks, Kade. So much. Just thanks."

"You are welcome, sunshine. Listen, this call is more for a favor, if you can do it." He already knew she could. "I need to be at a state realtor's banquet and wondered if you would be my plus one? This Sunday evening. Dinner is around six-thirty. Afterward is dancing."

"Umm, okay." She checked her work schedule on the wall. "Yes, I can accompany you. It sounds like fun."

"Good. I will have a car pick you up tomorrow. You need to buy a gown and shoes."

"Wait! What?"

"It's black tie, and I don't think it is right for you to pick up the cost, so I'm buying. I keep telling you I'm good for you. You just don't want to believe it. Bye, Domenica." *Click.*

As he slouched back into his couch, he thought about how his plan was working nicely so far. He had photographers lined up to take pictures of the two of them. He would have his PR people plaster the best ones in every newspaper and magazine that would publish them.

If Matt was keeping tabs—which he knew Matt was—he would see the pictures and return within a few days. He would figure that Domenica would be in danger from the OGA. He would also know that Kade Abraham was its acting agent. The best-case scenario would be that Matt would assume Domenica had fallen for him. That alone would have his ass back faster than anything else would. All Kade had to do was sit back and wait.

Kade stared out into space reflecting on many things: how he was a selfish bastard; how he wanted Domenica; how he would kill Matt and bury the body; how she would never find out; how she would fall in love with him eventually; how their first time would be. She *would* become his. All he had to do was kill Matt to move on to Nirvana. Christ, Masters was even paying him half a million for it.

"Yep, all I have to do is kill Matt. Fucking easy."

***

"Shopping!" The girls screamed in unison.

Kade's driver picked her up at exactly one o'clock with Shannon and Nikki in tow. She even had the list of stores he wanted her to browse through, the ones that only the rich frequented. The three girls were certainly in their glory. *Unique* was the fourth and final store they entered before a snack break, and Lord, was it! A pair of jeans ticketed at $1500!

"$1500! Just to put your ass in them!" Nikki exclaimed in amazement.

"Well, I don't need jeans." Domenica returned the beaded jeans to the rack. "Let's look at the gowns. Help me find something that says sophisticated-sexy."

"You mean you don't want your I'm-an-easy-slut-so-just-fuck-me style?" Nikki was in her prime today.

"No! God, Nikki. I just want to look nice for Kade, so he can be proud of his plus one." She held up a dress next to her in front of the full-length mirror. "I really don't want to be arrested for possible solicitation."

The girls burst into laughter as Domenica walked into a dressing room loaded with gowns. She tried dress after dress until both Shannon and Nikki screamed when she walked out in a black Venice lace-trimmed sheath with a side slit up to the hip.

In the back of the dress, the material draped around her shoulders flowing around the sides of her body leaving her muscular back on display. It culminated in a V just above her butt. The Venice lace appliqués had been applied strategically to give an ultra-feminine feel while the black color added that dab of sexy. The front dipped below the bust line held closed only by a tiny appliqué of black lace. The dress was stunning coming and going. Of course, the person who wore it had to have that perfect body, which Domenica possessed.

"Oh my God! That's it!" Shannon almost screamed her opinion aloud.

"That's the one! Get it! Get it!" Nikki followed.

"Hmm. I don't know… I think it's a bit—"

"Perfect!" the other two yelled out finishing her sentence.

"Kade doesn't have a chance," Nikki commented. "Name whatever you want, and it will be yours in that dress. How about trying for free rent for a year?"

Domenica glanced at the price tag wincing just a bit, but many of the others she tried on were even more expensive.

Shannon reminded her, "He said not to look at the price tag. Remember?"

"Yes. Okay. I'm getting this. If he is upset we can go shopping again tomorrow, I guess. What's great is that I can wear this with my black stilettos, and I have a red and crystal rhinestone jewelry set. I think I am ready to go!"

She finished her purchase, and the three girls loaded back up in the car to find a restaurant. After all, they just had to replenish their bodies after that difficult ordeal of shopping in the most exclusive stores in Atlanta.

When they returned to the apartment, she found a surprise waiting for her. Nikki and Shannon, who had run into Nikki's room ahead of her, suddenly were walking back out singing happy birthday to a twinkling one-candle cake.

"Wait a minute." Domenica pointed her finger up in the air as she called Kade. "Kade can you come down here for a piece of my birthday cake?"

"You said for a piece, Right?"

"At least you're consistent, Kade. I also said birthday cake!"

A few minutes later, he was walking in the door exclaiming, "I didn't buy you a gift, but I have a good excuse. I didn't know it was your birthday." A guilty look covered his face.

"Kade, are you crazy? That dress was twenty-three hundred dollars." After mentioning the price of the dress, she waited for his reaction.

"I told you not to worry about the price. Was that the dress you truly wanted, or did you buy it because it didn't cost as much as the others?"

"No! I really did like it. Shannon and Nikki both thought it looked good on me too. So I'm ready for your wining and dining adventure." Then she added, "And you are more than good for a birthday present. Probably for the next twelve years! Thanks, Kade."

"Great! Listen, don't get your hopes up that this is going to be some wonderful adventure." Kade informed her through swallows of cake. "It is dinner and a state meeting on rules and regulation changes for next year. Sometimes the others do not even hang around for the dancing.

"I don't care. At least, it is a place for me to go, something for me to do, even if I have to spend my time with a boring real estate agent." Domenica teased Kade quite relentlessly about his boring job. If she only knew.

"Oh, I bore you? I'll remember that the next time I think about sending you shopping. Listen, can I have my card. I don't want you to be bored buying other things with it."

Domenica laughed. "Yes. I'll go get it." She headed for her purse as Kade's phone rang.

"Ladies, this is business, and I'll have to take it upstairs," he told the girls as he quickly left the apartment. He saw who the call was from and let it go to voicemail as he took the elevator up to his place.

"I'll come up as soon as I find that damn card." She shuffled through her purse and emptied it out on the counter. When she finally found the card, she flew out the door and dashed up the stairwell, card in hand.

Chapter 18

Ding Dong. Kade opened the door, surprised that she followed him up so quickly. Domenica slipped in shutting the door behind her.

"Wow. I never knew a woman that gave a credit card back so fast."

"Shut up. I just did not want to be responsible for it. That's all." She handed the card to him.

Kade's fingers touched her fingers as he retrieved it. He slowly and purposefully entered her space. She backed into the closed door as he stealthily moved closer, his face so close, his nose brushing hers. He took a deep breath. Her smell consumed him. His hand slid up her arm while his other hand gracefully lowered settling on her waist. "Fuck, Domenica" he hoarsely whispered into her ear.

"Don't Kade." Her voice sounded raspy. Domenica turned her face, but no way could she control her body. Her breathing deepened as she placed her hands on his chest thinking she would push him away.

The essence of Kade surrounded her body. He was this turbulent vortex pulling her into his very being. Try as she might to fight it, he was a force no one could conquer. She slowly turned her face back to him, her nose gently rubbing his. Their eyes glued together.

Kade calmly placed his lips over hers. No matter how much she wanted to keep her distance, Kade was the human bandage protecting her fragile soul. There was no way she would strip him away. She kissed back, a gentle touch on his lips. He left her lips only to bestow baby kisses on her cheek, then the tip of her nose, then her other cheek, then back to her lips. His breathing altered. It deepened, it became brisk, it became heavy, uncontrolled. He tried to maintain gentleness, but desire took over. His dick hardened, his arms tightened around her, his tongue breached her lips to enter her mouth.

She reciprocated by deepening the kiss, reaching her hands around his neck, and sliding one up through his hair. The kiss elevated to a fury. When a dam breaks, all the water falls over with no cohesive plan to return. Her dam was shattering.

Kade had to take anything he could get. He might not have another chance. His hands started to feel every inch of her. He mentally had to take a snapshot of how she felt, in case this would be the last time he could ever touch her. He lived in the reality of the moment experiencing every second they clung to each other in their embrace, every movement she countered to his, every smell that exuded from her hair and her body, every touch that crept through his fingers to the sensory receptors in his brain. His tongue greedily tasted hers. He did not even close his eyes for a second to blink, worried that he would miss any of her reactions to him.

As though it had a mind of its own, his hand slid up under her top to the contour of her breast. He felt its heaviness. His thumb went to circle her nipple.

Ring!

Everything stopped.

Ring!

"Kade, stop. Please." She pulled back.

Ring!

"Answer your phone?"

"Fuuuuck!" Kade screamed out, pulling back from her to answer it.

"Did you kill the Motherfucker yet?" Colonel Masters asked in a harsh tone.

Kade started a slow walk away from Domenica lest she heard what he was saying. "Um, no. But it is as good as a done deal." He held up his index finger to Domenica wanting her to wait, but she responded by motioning she was leaving. She opened the door and quietly backed out of his apartment, waving slowly to him, blowing him a kiss as she closed his door.

"Has he even shown up yet?"

The Colonel is certainly impatient with this fucking contract. Kade held on to this thought.

"No and I told you this. The banquet is tomorrow so pictures won't even hit the paper until Monday or Tuesday. What the fuck!"

"Just making sure you don't lose sight, my boy. Don't. Lose. Sight!" *Click.*

That fucking son of a bitch just ruined his moment. *That cock blocker!* Kade threw his phone across the room knowing that someday he would have the privilege of killing the Colonel himself. One fucking shot between those beady eyes.

He sat on the couch, and then the strangest thought occurred to him. *Why does the Colonel want Matt dead so badly?*

Chapter 19

"Oh my God, you look stunning," Shannon squeaked as Domenica emerged from her room. Her hair ascended to the heavens with loose curls hanging and soft spiraling strands surrounding her face. That black dress molded to her body like a second skin. A smoldering charcoal smudge surrounded her bedroom eyes, and those full cherry-red lips just invited a sensuous kiss. The stiletto heels extended her long legs into outer space. She was an artist's masterpiece.

Shannon couldn't stop giggling.

"He doesn't have a chance tonight." Nikki smiled as she admired the work of art.

"Well, he wanted arm candy, he got arm candy. So I passed the test?"

The girls yelled out at the same time. "Oh yes!"

As the primping continued, Kade arrived knocking at their door. Nikki opened it wide to Kade's look of astonishment when he saw Domenica standing beside Nikki. There were quite a few seconds of mystified silence—as though what he was seeing was an illusion.

"Well? Do I pass?" Domenica's anxiety slowly crept over her as she turned around slowly.

"I, ah, I… I don't know what to say. I…" Kade took three steps forward, pulled her to him, and kissed her forehead. "You look too perfect, unbelievable. You look… Wow! Like a goddess come-to-life."

"You look gorgeously handsome in your tux too. You wear it well." Domenica felt this draw to his body as he held her close. Damn, she was in trouble tonight. She started to fantasize how he would probably wear naked very well too.

After he helped her into the limo, she became rather uncomfortable watching him stare at her. "Kade, please stop staring at me? It's making me self-conscious."

"It's just that you are truly perfectly beautiful. And I'm not saying that to get into those panties." He pulled her close and whispered in her ear. "By the way, if you tell me you aren't wearing any, this night will be one of my fantasies come to life."

She giggled. "I'm wearing them." She whispered back. "Sorry."

"Damn it!" He paused a moment pretending to be upset and then continued. "Did you ever see those black and white canvas paintings with one object in it emphasized in a bright color?"

She nodded yes.

"You are that bright color."

"Kade!" Domenica looked away turning red at the very masculine compliment.

"Kade, what is so special about me? I'm serious. What do you see in me?" She hoped he would say more than her looks. "And why do I seem to attract the…How do I say this? Guys like you. Maybe a bit on the bad-boy side."

He laughed at her last remark. "First off, what do I see in you? I'd like to see *me* in you, but you just are not accommodating."

"I knew you were going to go there as soon as I said it." She laughed at another very-Kade remark.

"I know this is not going to sound like an answer, but it is a great one, because it is why everyone is drawn to you." Here he paused again to say it right. "You. Are. You."

"What?"

"You're one of a kind! There's no other female like you. We, and by that I mean men, we can't group you anywhere. You are not the cheerleader type, the bimbo type, the intellectual, the nerd, the athlete, the I'm-gonna-save-the-planet Miss America type, the hard-core ghetto type. You are a little bit of everything put together—in a very nice package I might add." She listened intently. "Also with guys like me, you represent everything good. We bad boys just want to come home to that. We want to come home to good."

"Kade! I—"

"Wait. Hold up. One more thing." This time he spoke softly. "You are intriguing; a mystery to solve. I'm praying that someday you will let me try."

"Kade." She melted into him as they pulled up to the event.

"I'd like to peel all of your layers back from you to discover all of Domenica Bartholomew," he whispered in her ear adding in a serious tone, "But I'm afraid you're like peeling an onion. Once the layers are pulled away, I'll end up in tears." He quickly changed the subject. "Look! We're here."

As they exited the limo, he entwined her arm in his and sauntered into the building as though he were a king. He really did not need her as eye candy; he himself oozed virility that demanded attention from a room full of people.

Everyone turned to stare at the stunning couple walking into the banquet room.

When Kade saw the men slowly scrolling their eyes up and down Domenica, jealousy replaced pride. An innate animal instinct of my-territory, my-possession descended upon him. He pulled her in closer to him and grasped her hand tighter.

"Well, well, well. Kade Abraham. You have not been to these in a few years, but I see what brings you out these days. Who is this delight to the eyes?" A competitor in the city approached him.

"Hello, Jeremiah. Let me introduce you to my girlfriend. Domenica, Jeremiah. Jeremiah, Domenica."

"How are you?" Domenica cooed.

"As good as anyone can be in the presence of a goddess. I'm Jeremiah Ludwick, by the way." He took her hand and kissed it as he glared into her eyes.

Kade pulled her hand away. "She doesn't need to know your last name. She won't ever see you again." He addressed his next petulant remark to her. "Make sure all your fingers are still there," he said this loudly in front of Jeremiah.

As he led her away, a flutter of camera flashes sprinkled through the air. Kade pulled her closer and gave her a kiss on her cheek. "Smile pretty, baby girl."

"So I'm your girlfriend?" she whispered quietly to him.

"Tonight you are. Hey, let me enjoy my fantasy at least for one evening."

She smiled coyly and gently kissed his lips while the cameras sounded as though a myriad of cicadas were in the hall.

"What was that for?"

"Just because you are one amazing man." She walked with him to find their seats as the servers started to bring out the evening's entrees.

Just as Kade promised, the evening was boring as hell. Domenica did enjoy 'playing' Kade's girlfriend as nosey people asked how they met. She did not know how many times she described his act of heroism, catching her from her almost deadly fall on the dance floor. Of course, she accentuated the hand-on-the-boob part more than the catch itself. Everyone at the table howled, adding their own quips to the couple.

"Wow, so you really set a booby trap to get him?" one man asked.

"Kade, how did you keep abreast of that?" asked another.

And on and on, but Domenica noticed that Kade enjoyed being the brunt of *these* jokes especially when he realized, as she told the story, that the men slowly gazed down at her girls trying to be inconspicuous. All were wishing they could have been in his shoes, or in this case, be his hands.

"Come on. Let's dance." He pulled her up to the dance floor, the only couple up so far. He danced with her to his request, Mariah Carey's "Never Forget you" with Kade lip-syncing to the words.

As they danced, she stealthily took over the lead, pulling her knee sensuously up his leg, toe pointed, as she instructed him to dip her. He did slowly and then pulled her slowly back up to him. Next, she had him twirl her around just to meet his step as she returned to her position. They were small dance steps, but she knew how to make him look as though he had been dancing this way his whole life.

Everyone had their eyes on the perfect couple dancing. The couple so in love.

He wished they *were* in love. All he could think about was plowing his dick into her over and over later that night and in the morning. Hell, all the time!

At least all the cameras were taking their picture. A few would certainly make it in the major papers. They were *the* couple of the night. Maybe Matt would see just one of them. All he had to do was return, and Kade could solve all his problems: Kill Matt and Domenica would be his.

Not long now, dick, not long at all.

***

It was the following Sunday when Kade switched on the coffee pot and proceeded to his door, as he had done every morning since he moved in there. He grabbed the daily paper sitting pristinely on the floor and quickly perused the society section.

There it is—finally! After a whole fucking week it makes our paper! At least it made the major papers a few days after the event! Wow! On the front page, centered. A picture of Domenica and me with her body pulled in close to my body. He studied the picture in depth. *The photographer snapped it as she kissed me. It certainly looks like we are in love. God, she is beautiful. Hopefully, Matt saw it in a major paper this past week and interpreted the picture as a loving couple too. It wouldn't be long now.*

As he finished his coffee, he read the article. Then he went back into his room to shower and dress. He actually had real estate paperwork to do today so he was off to his office. A floor below, Domenica also carried a cup of coffee in her hand as she once again described that night's events to Shannon. Both girls were living vicariously through her. Well, maybe not Nikki.

"Kade is amazing." Domenica sighed.

"I can't deny that. He looked like the dream prince every girl wants. I still don't understand why you aren't dating him, and by that, I mean fucking him. God. All he'd have to do is stare at me with those dark eyes, and I think I would climax!" Seated at the table, Shannon plopped her elbow on the table and placed her head in her palm staring out the window, probably visualizing fantasies of Kade and her.

"This is why I am so confused. The last few weeks I have been having dreams about Kade instead of Matt. I feel so guilty."

"Oh, you poor thing. Hunky Kade instead of Hottie Matt. Wow! I really feel sorry for you. Such a terrible dilemma for a girl to be in."

Domenica slapped her playfully. "You know what I mean." She was smiling, but suddenly she became very serious. "I love Matt. But now, I think I love Kade too. How can I love two men? That's not right. It's just not."

"I'm just saying I would love to have your problem for just one day." Shannon reiterated.

"No, you wouldn't. Listen, I have to go meet up with Nikki." Domenica left Shannon sitting at the table, "We have practice, and then both of us are going to hit the weight room. We want to do some extra lifting today. I'll see you later. I'll need the washer later so if you need to use it, do it while I'm out. Bye guuurlfriend!" She collected her gym bag and was off to work off some of her woes.

"Hey! I won't be here when you get back. Gotta go to the real library to work on a paper. Have fun." Shannon called out.

Chapter 20

A few hours later, Domenica was opening her door and throwing her stuff on the little table to the right of the door. "Shannon? Shannon? Good, she's not here either." She walked into her apartment. "I can get a lot of stuff done and—"

Suddenly from behind the door, a massive body overpowered her, pulling her into it as a hand simultaneously clasped over her mouth. She tried to scream and started to go into a position to throw her assailant until she heard the magic words.

"Domenica! It's me!" Her body relaxed, and he let go of her.

She whirled around to face him. "Matt!" She fell into his body and started to sob. "Matt," she cried out through her tears. "Matt. I thought I'd never see you again. I thought you were dead." She broke down in his arms as he tried to console her.

Matt whispered in her ear. "Domenica, shh. It's okay. I'm here. I'm back for a while." He pressed his lips to hers, gently at first, but then their passion kicked into gear until Domenica realized what she had heard.

She pulled back to look into his eyes. "For a while? What do you mean, for a while?" He separated from her and turned around, walking to the window to stare out at the sky. With one hand on his hip and the other roughly plowing through his hair, he continued. "I was on my way to take care of my problem, but I had to come back here to see you. To make sure you were okay. I… I know you are naïve to some of the evil in the world… but I saw pictures of you… I saw… Is there…" He did not know how to proceed with what he needed to find out, what he had to ask her. "Did you move on?"

"What? Move where?" She could not understand. To the new apartment? Where was he going with this?

"Did you…?" Matt's primitive animal side quickly seized his logical brain. Monstrous jealously controlled and consumed him. He turned abruptly to face her. "Did you fuck Kade?"

She stood there, her mouth agape. Once again, she was that little puppy that did not quite understand its owner's commands with head tilted to the right. Did she what?

The confused silence lasted for a few seconds, and then an epiphany emerged out of her confusion.

"Wait! You *know* Kade?"

"Did you fuck him? Are you and he …a couple? Are we done?"

If one holds a lighted match at the bottom of a piece of paper, the fire spirals up that paper consuming it, leaving nothing but black flakey ashes. Fueling the emotion from within was a flame of burning anger that started in her toes and quickly consumed her body as it travelled to her brain.

She talked to him with formidable precision. "You have been gone for months while I have been trying to keep it together both physically and mentally. I've lost concentration. I've lost sleep. Christ, I've lost weight." She took a deep breath trying to keep control. "My grade point average dropped. I even lost some friends who argued with me that I should forget about you. I actually quit hanging around with them."

She tried to control that Italian temper. "I have been living day to day in loneliness and grief." Now, she started to walk toward him.

That Italian temper won. The embers in the ash reignited. She lifted her finger poking it ferociously into his chest with each emphatic word of her next statement. "And the first thing you want to know is if I. Fucked. Someone. Else?"

"Domenica, please. That picture killed me. I just—"

"You just want to know if your property is tarnished. If someone else took your toy out of the sandbox and played with it!" She collected her thoughts for a moment, and then slammed her hands into his chest with her next question. "How do you know Kade?" He caught his balance as he fell back into the wall.

"He and I work in the same OGA. He is probably here to find out what you know about me. He might even be the one with the contract to kill me. You are in danger, Domenica. That's why I'm back."

"Oh, *now* you are worried about me." She turned from Matt. Abruptly, it all made sense. Kade suddenly coming into her life, Kade wanting to know about her relationship with Matt, and, what hurt the most, Kade deceiving her. He *didn't* love her. He just wanted Matt. "That fucker! That low-life, motherfucking, fucking asshole fucker! Fuuuuck!" She turned back to Matt. "Get out!" She shoved him to her door.

"Domenica, I came back to protect you!"

She opened the door. "Get out! Now!" She shoved him again harder this time.

"Please Domenica! He kills people!"

"So. Do. You! You motherfucker! Get the fuck out!' She was about to push him out when he grabbed her and shook her.

"Domenica! I. Love. You!"

Slap! Right across his face.

"Too late for those words now." She pushed him away, stood still a moment taking a deep breath, and looked up at him, emphatically saying, "Get! Out!"

He slipped her a piece of paper. "My phone number is on there if you need to get in touch with me." She would not look at him.

He waited. He turned. Finally, he left. She slammed her door closed.

Domenica leaned back against her door with her scrambled thoughts taking over. *This can't be real. Maybe this is a nightmare. No, it can't be a nightmare, because a person awakens from a nightmare.* She knew what she was going to do next.

Opening the door, she didn't even wait for the elevator. She ran up the stairwell, pounded on Kade's door, and waited. One, two, three, four. She pounded again and waited. One, two, three, four. She raised her arm to pound again. The door slowly creaked open.

"Domenica! To what do I owe this lovely surpr—?"

He didn't even see the right hook as it plowed into his face. Starting with his head, his body performed a perfect body roll as he crashed to the floor.

"Fuck! You! You motherfucker!" she screamed at him, as he caressed his sore jaw and looked up at her. She turned in a huff and stomped off.

Kade's confused eyes followed her, and then a realization hit him almost as hard as she did. "What do you know about that? Matt's back."

***

"I am going to kill both of them, Nikki."

"Hold on. All you did was cry cuz he was gone, and now he's back, and you are going to kill him?" Nikki was confused.

"He came back because he thinks I'm sleeping with Kade. That fucker! I may just go into his line of work. Just. One. Time. Wait! Maybe *two* times!"

"Okay, so now you are killing Kade too?" Nikki prodded her to go on.

"Kade was here to find out about Matt. He set me up! Maybe I am naïve. Maybe I'm just stupid when it comes to men."

"Oh, aren't we all!" Nikki flapped her hand back and forth and pretended to move on.

"Listen, let's just change the subject. I was taught not to talk ill of the soon-to-be dead." Domenica tried to smile, but the tears just started to fall down her cheeks.

The two men in her life played her for a fool. One was more concerned with his pride, meaning his dick. The other had her believing there might be something wonderful between them when there was absolutely nothing. So Kade might kill her? The problem was that if that happened, she would probably still die loving both of them.

Wait! I loved both of them? My God, I do!

She was an idiot! To think she missed Matt so much that she allowed it to affect her mental and physical being. The sad thing she realized now was that maybe she only missed the man she *thought* he was.

As for Kade, she would never forgive him. Never! He took advantage of her in her state of darkness. How could he do that? How could he? Tears flooded her eyes again.

"Domenica. Maybe you should talk to them one at a time and see what their side is. I am good at deciphering men, and I can't believe that neither loved you. Even Kade. He isn't even on earth when you're around. He floats above the ground somewhere. Just talk to each of them. Even if it's for you to find closure."

"I'll think about it. Right now, I have to get ready for work. Put my life on hold from these two assholes and work and go on as if nothing is wrong. Just like before. I fucking hate men!" She went into her room, slamming the door shut to change for work. "Fucking men," she murmured.

Chapter 21

"So did the fucker show up yet?" Colonel Masters had Kade stewing on his end of the conversation. Masters was like the annoying alarm clock that buzzed right in the middle of a wonderfully erotic dream. The alarm clock he always threw at the wall and broke.

"No, but the picture just appeared in the paper last weekend. So it's been only about a week and a half." Kade sat on his couch, the phone coddled between his ear and shoulder. He now realized he needed time to think before he went off killing Lima Bean. Kade kept thinking how Masters had wanted this contract to be completed a little too quickly. Like two weeks ago too quickly!

"And I told you that you are out of time. I want results by the end of *this* week!" Masters slammed his phone down again in Kade's ear. Then, the Colonel sucked in a few puffs on his cigar and stared out of his office window in his reflective mode.

Suddenly he dialed another number. "Yes. Can you get to Atlanta in a few days? I have a duel job I think you would be interested in doing... Of course, double the money...a few enemies of the state. Traitors."

While Colonel Masters finished that phone call, Kade was busy opening his safe to pull out a smaller gun he would now wear around his ankle. Two should be enough. Since Lima Bean now knew that Masters hired Kade to kill him, friendship of any kind was out the window. Kade would have to be even more aware of his surroundings every second he left his apartment.

Right now, he had to figure out a way to convince Domenica to talk to him. Before, it would never have been important if one of the women he hooked up with walked out on him. He never allowed anyone to have this much of an effect on him. He realized that with Domenica there was no *allowing* about it. It was not a matter of choice; it just happened. She was this force of nature passing over his life and taking him along for the turbulent ride.

If she walked out on him? That would destroy him. Just his wanting her caused a physical pain in his core. He thought about the first time he saw her; it was this euphoric surrender of his entire being to her. At first, he thought about her a few times a day during his quiet reflective moments, but that morphed into her controlling his every thought. In fact, thinking about her became a physical need for him to survive.

There were days he performed his daily duties while thinking one hundred per cent of her. He didn't know if reports he wrote for his business were correct. He didn't even care if they were correct. It came to be that she was the only thing important to his existence. She was his fix. And he would do anything to get that fix. Lie, cheat, steal, and even murder.

What would it be like if he never talked to her again, or touched her, or smelled her, or saw her? He never ever wanted to find out. Lord knows he felt her even when she wasn't there, but he also had to see her. If not, his body experienced symptoms of withdrawing from the most potent drug of all. Yes, he yearned for her, and it was the most wonderfully devastating component of his whole existence.

Certainly, that first infatuation was now an incurable addiction. He hungered for her, actually craved her! He hated her when she wouldn't give in, but covered this emotion in front of her, so she wouldn't become angry with him. Because *that* might cause her to leave him. God, she made him a sniveling coward, and she didn't even know she did this to him! A few days without her and he endured restless sleeps, a lack of concentration, anxiety, and even a loss of appetite.

The worst thing he had to endure was that hopelessness that shrouded him, smothering his very soul when she wasn't around. Although he wanted more physically, the little that he got at least made life bearable, even if it was only a text or phone call to hear her voice or a quick visit to her door with a lame excuse to see her.

The stupidest thing he did was actually invent scenarios that he tried to act out. What he would say to her at dinner, and what her response might be so he could have the perfect answer to impress her. Where she might be, so he could meet up with her *coincidentally*. Stupid, fucking humiliating shit like that. He realized that without her knowing it, she totally controlled his heart and mind. How could he ever feel for someone else the same powerful intensity that he had for her?

Away from her these past few days? He was this love-junkie. She was the fix. He didn't want less of her; he needed more.

Domenica Bartholomew. The missing piece to his life that he had to place into the rest of the pieces to finish his life's puzzle. He just had to convince her of that and survive Matt Lima Bean Hoover.

***

The first day of September brought an upbeat knocking on Domenica's door. She did not even have to look through the peephole; she knew that beat. She opened the door and lunged into his huge arms hugging him tight. "Well, well, well. How are you, stranger?"

"Hey, hey, hey! Whazzup?" Six foot five Jamal towered in front of her.

"To what do I owe this honor? You are never home. You don't answer my calls."

"I been busy. I'm kinda seein' a beautiful lady," Jamal embarrassingly admitted.

"What?" Domenica could not hide her shock. "The playa' ain't playin' no mo'?"

"I'm kinda tryin' out this relationship shit," Jamal answered.

"Well, if you are calling it shit, I'm afraid it's doomed already. Do you need to talk about it?" Domenica and Jamal were always there for each other, no matter how busy they were in their lives.

"No, I really came to deliver a message." He looked around and bent to whisper in her ear. "Is it safe to talk in here?"

Domenica knew right away to what he was referring. "So he is staying with you and Dawan?"

"Yeah. Domenica. You gotta talk to him. He's hurtin' real bad over your fight. Come over pretending to visit me and just listen to him, okay?"

Domenica turned from Jamal walking away. "I can't believe this. Did he tell you what we fought about?"

"Hey, I ain't gittin' in nobody's business. All I know is the boy is hurtin'.'"

"We haven't seen each other for all these months, and the first thing he wants to know is if I'm fucking Kade. He *knew* Kade! They work for the same OGA!"

"Whoa! Shit!" Jamal now realized the bad situation he just put himself into. Then the political side of him kicked in. "Domenica, I ain't tellin' you yo' business, but shouldn't you just give him a chance? Or don't you love him no more? What is talkin' gonna hurt?"

Reflecting for a moment on what Jamal said to her, she answered him. "You are right. I need to see what's going on before I make a decision." She turned toward Jamal. "Jamal, I'm going to give you some advice. Before you whisper words of love to this lady of yours, make sure you see all of her."

"I *been* seein' all of her!" Jamal lifted his brows waggling them with a devilish look on his face.

Domenica had to laugh. "I don't mean that. I mean after the 'perfect' wears off. When that happens, and the infatuation is gone, you see without the blinders hiding the *ugly*. My blinders were ripped off by the two men I thought I loved." She reflected a minute and added, "I thought the pain was bad when Matt left. But let me tell you, the pain from betrayal is ten times worse." She wiped the tears off her cheeks as she went to her couch to sit.

Jamal crossed over to her placing his hand on her shoulder. "You know I'm here for you, baby girl. Any time you need to talk. You know I love you. But just come over and listen to him. He's at my place, so just pretend you're visitin' me."

"I will. Later today. I just need to compose myself before I have that conversation. At least my eyes will be wide open this time."

"If you walk over with me now, I can be your support. Come on. Let's get this over with. You, me, helpin' each other. Like old times."

Domenica thought awhile and then declared, "You are right. No use running away from a situation."

Chapter 22

The walk to the old apartment building was quicker than she wanted it to be. They went into the building and took the steps to Jamal's floor. He opened the door. There, sitting on the couch was Matt who turned to them, a little surprised to see Domenica standing there. She walked over and sat beside him.

"Hi, Matt."

"Domenica," He nodded warily.

It was amazing that after all they'd been through, after all the initial infatuation, after all the love, after all the desire, after all the situations that made them protect each other, after all of that, they did not know what to say to each other. They sat there not even looking at each other. Distant. Cold.

Jamal rescued them from the extreme silence. "I'll just go in the other room so's you two can discuss your problems." He walked away leaving them alone.

"Domenica, I—"

"Matt, I—" they said in unison.

After a deep breath, she let Matt start. "I apologize for my comment about you and Kade. I want you to realize that I was going crazy with so much jealousy that I allowed it to control me. I know you are not the kind of person to jump from one man to another to another. Please forgive me, Domenica, please."

Then, it was Domenica's turn. She took a deep breath. "Matt, I went through a lot when you left. You have to understand I never loved anyone the way I loved you." Matt shuddered at her use of the past tense of love. "I thought you were the one."

"And now?" Matt held his breath. He could not interpret from her words or actions where this was going.

"I don't know. You and Kade put me in this situation. I don't trust either of you. I'm in a self-preservation mode. Either of you can destroy me—*if* I allow it."

Matt kept quiet for a moment thinking about what he would say. Then he started. "All I know is that I love you. I would die for you, Domenica. I was on my way to kill my boss so you would be safe. And yes, it is that serious," he added when he saw her reaction to his last statement. "When I saw Kade, I knew he was the one sent to kill me, and I assumed he would kill you, too. But after studying that picture, I knew the look he had for you was not one of murder, but one of love. He loves you, doesn't he?"

"Yes." Her answer was to the point.

"I'm not trying to accuse you of anything, but do you love him?"

Domenica was quiet.

"That's what I thought." Matt turned away from her for a few seconds, took a deep breath, and then turned back to face her once more.

"You don't know anything," Domenica retorted in defense mode, the volume in her voice rising. She stopped to change her whole approach. She paused a few seconds to collect her thoughts. "This is what I mean about both of you!" She looked into Matt's eyes. "The two of you both talk like this is something I caused. You came into *my* life. Kade came into *my* life. I didn't choose *you* two, you both chose *me*. Now I am the one who has to solve this problem? No! It is not going to be me. You need to find Kade and, without killing each other, you both need to solve the primary problem first. You both need to get out of the killing business. Because I'm not going to be with anyone who thinks that killing is okay. Legal or not!"

She stood. Her insides were actually quivering. Matt stood up and tried to pull her into him. "No!" She screamed out, pushing away from him. "There is no more of us until the problem is solved."

"Domenica, please."

"Good-bye, Matt" She walked to the door remembering the last time she left, after their lovemaking in Jamal's apartment, when he left to board the bus. This time she walked out without even looking back.

Now to Kade's to tell him the same thing. Somebody had to face the situation and solve it. "I guess that's me," she said after she slammed the door.

***

She made the walk home in an instant and in seconds, she was in front of Kade's apartment. She knocked, heard shuffling inside, and instantly saw that ethereal face smiling at her as he answered the door.

"Domenica, I can explain. Please give me a chance to explain." He pulled her into his place before she could change her mind and leave.

"There seems to be a lot of explaining going on today. Okay. Let me hear it." She sat at his kitchen counter. She noticed he had a gun hidden behind his back, "Are you going to shoot me if I refuse your explanation?" she sarcastically asked as she pointed to the gun.

"Now you're being silly. This gun is if Matt or someone I don't know shows up. You see, because I did not fulfill the contract to kill Matt yet, I probably have one out on me. Or I'll just have Matt shooting at me." He put the gun down on his kitchen table and placed his hand over hers. "Domenica, I would never hurt you. I told you I love you. That was the truth. I. Love. You. I know you don't feel the same, but it doesn't matter. You are the only good thing that has come out of this whole mess. The only good thing that was ever in my life."

"That's not true, Kade. I do love you. Remember? Ti amo."

"Domenica!" Kade rushed to hold her.

"Hold up!" She pushed him away. "I was just with Matt, and I'm telling you the same thing I told him. I didn't cause this situation. I didn't choose you. You chose me. You need to meet with Matt and figure out how you are going to solve this killing business without killing each other. I am *not* going to be with anyone who has a resume filled with a list of dead people. Not happening."

Kade studied her quietly for a while. She totally controlled him. Probably controlled Matt too. And, they both would crawl to her to do whatever she demanded. Christ. They were the two pussies in this relationship, not her. "Okay, I'll meet with him, but you have to be there, so he doesn't try to kill me. If you are there, he won't shoot me, and I won't shoot him."

"Okay. I'll set it up. Oh and Kade. If you renege on this and try to kill him, I will kill you. Got it?" She was serious.

"I got it." He went to pull her to him, but she rose quickly and backed away.

"I'll call you when everything is set up." She hastened to the door to leave.

Domenica?" he called after her. She turned to look at him. "Do you really love me?"

"Yes, Kade. I love both of you. Crazy, huh? I mean, how could I not? Both of you are amazing."

He watched her turn and walk out the door. In fact, he watched until she faded into the elevator. As she did, he whispered, "*Ti amo*, Domenica. *Ti amo*."

***

It took Domenica a week to set everything up. She knew the meeting would have to be in a somewhat public area so both Matt and Kade would have to control their actions. This way there was a smaller chance to alarm or harm innocent people. She picked the perfect spot in The Library, and John didn't even question what she needed his back storage room for when she asked to use it for a few hours. Yesterday, she went in to set up a small square table with two chairs around it and made sure the lighting was bright enough. She already sent a message to Matt and Kade with their positive response about the location and time of the meeting at The Library. Now at home, sitting on her couch, she watched the time tick by slowly.

Shannon emerged from the bathroom wrapped in a towel.

"Are you getting ready for a date?" Domenica asked.

Shannon laughed. "Are you kidding? Remember. I'm the dumb one of the three amigas! I'm off to the real library. I have to keep my face in a book studying, if I'm not working. And that merits me some A's and B's and sometimes a C or D. I did not believe college would be so hard."

"It becomes a bit easier when you figure out which professors to pick and how to write for each of their personalities. Did I tell you about my first year when the prof for my first writing class gave me a D on my first paper? If you remember, I *was* valedictorian and I *did* win prizes in writing contests. And *every* English teacher I had in high school told me I should become a writer. An older girl in the class that I partnered with for projects told me Professor Jennings was into gardening and flowers." Domenica reflected back into that first year. "She said to somehow incorporate gardening and flowers into my papers."

"Did it work?"

"My next paper was a descriptive paper on how I helped Mom in her garden, and how that brought us closer together."

"Your mom had a garden?"

"Nope."

"But your paper—"

"You and I know that. She didn't!"

"Wait! An A?"

"An A!

"That is actually good advice. Hmm, write what they want to hear." She started to throw on her sweats and tank top as she waltzed to the door. "I know you are off tonight, but are you going to The Library later?"

"I'll be there somewhere," Domenica called out as Shannon slammed the door behind her.

Domenica sat back on the couch remembering how at the beginning of last school year she worried how Jamal, Dawan, Nikki, and Shannon knew about Matt and a little about Kade. It was best to keep everyone on a need to know basis. What Matt, Kade, and she were dealing with now was dangerous. If what Matt told her was true, this Colonel Masters was no joke.

How sad. She used the word *if.* Before he left, she believed everything he said. Now, she doubted everything he said. She glanced at the time. Not too long now, not too long at all.

Chapter 23

Domenica heard the squeaking of the door hinges as she turned the knob and pushed the storage room door open. She flipped on the light switch, gently closing the door behind her. While she waited for them, she decided to walk around the table and straighten the chairs. As she bent down to reach for the other chair, she thought how it smelled like Kade in here. *Hmm, that's weird.*

Gruffly, a hand wrapped around her waist while the other clamped down on her mouth. "Don't scream. It's me."

She recognized Kade's voice immediately. She grabbed his one arm, twisted around with it, and in no time had it bent up behind him—to his amazement.

"How the fuck did you do that?"

"How the fuck did you get in here without being seen."

"I stay alive because I'm that good."

Domenica released his arm. "I'm not playing, Kade. Just know I'm not playing."

"I'd still rather wait by these shelves just in case Matt comes in shooting." He moved back to the shelves as his eyes danced up and down her body.

Domenica went back to the chair nervously straightening it out.

The silence in the room was deafening. "I thought I'd come early so we could talk about—"

"Shut up, Kade." She didn't even look at him.

Silence. The minutes acted like snails nonchalantly maneuvering as though they had no specific place to go, no specific time to be anywhere, no specific reason to move quickly.

Knock, knock, knock.

Finally.

Domenica peered through the crack she made in the door while Matt nervously looked up and down the hall. She opened the door wide for him to enter. As he came in, he positioned his hand to be ready to use his gun.

Kade stared at Matt; Matt stared at Kade. They looked like two gamecocks just placed in a cockpit waiting to fight, but with hidden guns as their metal spurs. She knew they both were carrying. That was something neither would give up.

Matt broke the silence greeting his adversary. "Kade."

"Lima Bean."

"Lima Bean?" Domenica echoed.

"Long story." Matt answered her, never taking his eyes off Kade.

"Let's not drag this out. Domenica wants us to settle the situation. I think that's how she said it." Kade stared at Matt.

"I just want to know why you took the contract. I thought we were friends." Matt's pitch raised on the last word.

"Hey, I don't care if it's my own fucking mother. If you are a traitor to this country, I will take that person out."

"Wait. What do you mean a traitor?" Matt's confusion was evident.

"Hold on a second." Kade walked to the door, opened it, and looked out to see if anyone could hear what he was saying. No one there. All he heard was the muffled sounds of music. "There would not be a contract on you if you didn't do something illegal. What was it? Did you kill someone at a bar fight and try to cover it up? Did you sell our organization out to a foreign country? Did you need lots of money to impress a certain young lady?" Domenica even glared at him with anger to that last remark.

Matt started toward Kade, hands ready to swing, but Domenica came between. "Both of you sit!" They paused. "I. Said. Sit." They responded by sitting at the same time to where she designated. "Matt, is this true? Did you do anything illegal?" After all the lies that he told her, how could she even believe him now?

Matt clasped his hands together on top of the table. "Kade, I don't know what bullshit Masters filled your head with, but nothing like that happened."

He proceeded to tell Kade about the sanctioned hit of the young mother in Florida. "She was innocent, Kade. I shot her with her little boy watching. Right between the eyes."

This time he rose and walked to face the door hiding the emotions that were still evident through his quivering voice. He turned quickly on Kade, this time pounding his fist into the table.

"I still wake up in the night seeing that little boy's face, hearing him call out to his mother!" Matt took another second to compose himself. "I don't care what you do, but I'm never killing anyone again unless it is to defend myself. And I will defend myself, Kade, even against someone I thought was like a brother to me."

He sat down again adding, "I will also defend Domenica, since I know Colonel Masters will never let her live. You know how he ties up loose ends. Go ahead. Check my story out. You know you have the means to do so."

Kade lifted his hand and rubbed his fingers against his chin as if reflecting on Matt's story. "Oh, I will do that. And I will tell you I am leaning towards believing you."

"I think what set Masters off was when I threatened him that I'd go to the press. I realized why he has such a great record in the finding-and-killing American enemies. He uses anything and anyone to achieve his goal. I just wonder how many more of us have killed an innocent person so he could get at the criminal. How many have you killed, Kade?"

Kade grew silent then added, "I never even questioned any of my hits. Just did the deed and watched my bank account grow."

A deep feeling of guilt suddenly swept over him.

"Don't think you are alone. I did the same thing, and if her child wasn't with her, I probably would have figured she was an enemy of the state too."

"How'd you find out?"

"That motherfucker actually thought he was consoling me when he admitted she was shot only to draw her husband into the country, so he could be taken out. As soon as he said it, I think he realized that he admitted to an unsanctioned killing. A murder he ordered. How many more has he been responsible for?"

"Fuck." Kade pushed back from the table. "Domenica, I need to talk to Lima Bean alone. Could you go somewhere for about ten minutes?"

"No."

Matt asked her next.

"Domenica, this will be classified stuff we will be discussing, and I think Kade now understands that the contract on me is to hide Masters' crimes, not mine. Trust us please. Can you please step out and go for a walk?"

Reluctantly, she left the room. Matt peered out the door to make sure she was gone then turned to Kade. "What are we going to do? You know by taking this contract you signed your own death warrant. He leaves no loose ends. That means Domenica and you too."

"Yes, my dear Lima Bean, I am now certain of that. My guard went up when he was too eager to get rid of you. You got any ideas?"

"Actually, yes. I was on my way to DC when I saw that picture. Good ploy, by the way, to draw me out."

Kade shrewdly smiled. "Hey. We all know a man's weakness is his dick. Do go on."

"Colonel Masters only keeps the files of his assassins, us and a few others, on his office computer. So that's the only one he'd have to destroy if it came down to erasing incriminating information. I thought I could get into the building, infiltrate his office, and destroy it. That erases me, you, and everyone else. No records, no assassins. Then, Kade. I. Am. Taking. Him. Out."

The hatred in Matt's eyes glared out of his sockets like lasers. "I have to protect Domenica."

"Sounds like a decent plan. Count me in. Tomorrow we can leave. Right outside of DC is a dive motel where we can stay and plan everything. What's the name of it again? Red Sunset!"

Kade was ready for this. He would give his life protecting Domenica too.

"Shall we call her back in and tell her we kissed and made up?"

Kade reached his hand out to shake with Matt. Matt reciprocated. Done deal. They started planning to leave early the next morning for their ten-hour drive to Washington DC.

Chapter 24

After driving all day, they were almost to their destination as Kade stretched his legs again. He thought about what they had planned so far. The only thing in their favor was the fact that the Colonel would never dream that *anyone* would attempt to infiltrate the United States Environmental Action Alliance building. Christ, even the name of the OGA had Kade believing it was for the good of the country. Hopefully, the element of surprise, along with each of their talents, would help them succeed.

Kade broke the silence as Matt continued driving toward DC. "I think we should take him out at his home. What if he has files on his home computer? I could make it look like a suicide."

"That might not be a bad idea. That means I would have to be in his office while you are in his home. I've been studying the layout of the building for a few months now, especially the venting system. Unless they have reconstructed everything, I could probably crawl to his office with my eyes shut. I can also go in as a technician to fix something. I'll figure it out."

"That means we are going to need a few more people to help. I have one who could be my driver and backup. You remember LL, right?"

Matt smiled. How could anyone forget the worst white rapper ever? "Yeah, I remember him. I'll call the other three men that you saved along with me. They told me if you ever needed anything at all to just call. I'm sure a couple of them will be willing to help.

"Who is it?"

"Darrell is the greatest computer hacker I've ever met. Peewee started drag racing as a teen, and he still dabbles in it. He can be a driver. Mike is probably better than both you and me in the shooting department, and actually works for Colonel Masters too. I told him to apply, and they recruited him too. So another one who knows the ins and outs of the OGA building. All of us still train in the martial arts."

"You better get in touch with Mike and warn him about Masters. Hey, it's starting to get dark outside." Kade looked at his watch and then looked up to notice a sign for an upcoming motel. "This is the place I was telling you about. We should stop here." As Matt pulled into the parking lot, Kade perused the old building. "Christ! It looks like only dirt bags would stay here."

"You mean like us?"

"Yep. Just like us." Kade laughed as Matt dropped him off in front of the office doors while he parked in the back between two trucks. Kade flipped down cash to pay for the room, grabbed the keys from the manager, and walked out to the back of the motel where their room was located.

Matt took a quick shower before he plummeted into the depths of the old mattress to try to doze off into the long, deep sleep he so desperately needed. Kade walked toward the bathroom to shower next when he heard steps outside their door. Tension in both of them escalated as he quickly waved to Matt and pointed to the door. Matt was up and alert now, stealthily grabbing his gun off the bedside table.

Kade slowly tiptoed to his jacket retrieving his gun, and then tiptoed to the door just as someone knocked on it. With gun drawn while motioning for Matt to cover him, he turned the knob.

In a flash, he pulled the door open and grabbed the invader. Matt jumped up next to him to help subdue the enemy who emitted a high shriek. "Eeeek!"

Both Kade and Matt called out in unison, "Domenica?"

"What the fuck are you doing here?" Kade yelled at her as he threw her on the bed.

"I know what you are planning. The kitchen is on the other side of the storage room wall, and you can hear everything that goes on in that room. I'm going with you."

No, you're not!" Matt yelled out.

"You are *not!*" Kade reiterated angrily.

"Yes. I am!" She said with a smile. She sat on one of the beds and bounced on it. "I'll take this one; you and Kade will have to share a bed." She put her backpack on the side of her bed and laid back into the pillow.

"You're not going with us." Matt exerted.

"Neither of you have any right to tell me what to do. Both of you got me into this mess. I'll help get us out. I'm turning in early. Good night, sweet dreams." She rolled over, her back to them.

Kade and Matt stared at each other with Kade finally saying, "You can't win with her. Believe me I've tried." He didn't even try to fight this battle. He walked past her into the bathroom to shower as Matt started to plead with her.

"Domenica."

She rolled back to look at him.

"Please don't do this. If anything happened to you, I—"

"Matt, I think you should shut up and get some sleep." She rolled back to face the wall.

He plopped down on his bed observing the curve of her waist to her hip. "Okay then." Matt said in a huff. That ass was just there waiting for him to take it, except he couldn't.

Yeah, get some fucking sleep. Little chance of that with her in the room.

He rolled over, pounded his hand in one of the pillows, and faced the opposite wall.

Domenica smiled until Kade came out of the bathroom with just a scanty towel around his waist. Of course, it had to dip lower in the front. She propped herself up. *God, he's so fucking hot. Sexy just oozes out of every one of Kade's pores.*

Here she was, in a motel room with not one but two hot men, and there would be nothing going on with either of them.

"Couldn't you please finish dressing in the bathroom?" she asked quite irritated.

"See something you like?" Kade just had to tease her. "Hey. You wanna play with the big boys; you play by their game rules. *You* go in the bathroom while *I* change where I'm comfortable!" She rolled over to face the wall again just as he dropped his towel and slid on his boxers.

Fucking men! They're all assholes!

"You know, to pass the time, we could have a threesome," Kade flippantly verbalized.

"Shut up, Kade," Domenica and Matt responded with Domenica throwing a pillow at his head.

"Just a thought! You know, to ease the tension in the room."

"Shut up, Kade," Domenica and Matt responded with Matt throwing a pillow this time.

"Okay! Okay! I get it. Everyone's too tired right now." Kade switched off the dresser light and continued. "Maybe later?" The other two simultaneously pounded their fists into their pillow and plopped their heads down. "I will sleep in the chair. No offense, Matt, but I don't want my dangling guys anywhere near your dangling guys." With that, he picked up the two tossed pillows and slouched into the chair covering himself with one of the bedspreads.

***

The eight hours of sleep felt like one hour as Domenica opened her tired eyes to the first ray of sunlight lightly sweeping across her face. She rolled over stretching her arms into the air and hit into...

Wait! What the hell is lumped against me? "Kade! What the fuck?" She yelled pushing her feet into his back until he almost rolled off the bed.

"Hey. I needed to sleep, and the chair was not doing it for me."

"So you crawled in with me?"

"Did I wake you? No! Was I going to sleep with a man? No!"

Matt jumped up at the commotion and stood face to face with Kade, jealous anger quickly filling him. "If I didn't need you for this job, I'd fucking kill you right now."

Kade was in his face in a second, "You could try, Lima Bean. You could try."

Domenica quickly pushed between them. "Let me make this clear again! I do not belong to either of you. So quit acting like two bucks in rutting season. Got it? Go piss out your territories somewhere else!"

Kade and Matt coldly stared at each other.

"I said 'got it?' I don't need any more territorial man-pee dripping down my leg!"

"Yeah, got it," they echoed in unison.

"Kade, can you go and get us some breakfast?" He did not move. "Please?" Kade didn't answer as he threw on some clothes, grabbed his wallet, and slammed the door on his way out.

"Matt," she turned on him and exploded. "Do not think that I am back with you. Do not think I am here because of you. Do not think that because of our past, you can tell me what to do." As she emphasized her concerns, she plowed her index finger into his sternum—again. "Do not think that you own me. No one does. Not you. Not Kade. Nobody. Got it?"

"Domenica, I love you."

"Then you should have been up front with me from the beginning. The way I see it, we are all in this because of you. I'm here now, in danger, because of your decisions."

She might as well have slapped him in the face—again. There it was. The truth. She blamed him. And she was right. He was selfish. He wanted her and instead of doing what was right, quitting his job first and then coming back to her, he just went after what he wanted, not giving her a chance to decide if she would want to be with someone like him. Now, because of his selfishness, she, her friends, and family were all in danger. If he and Kade did not get rid of those files and kill Masters, they all might die anyway.

"I'm going to shower. Don't think that you are welcome to take one with me. You are not."

"Domenica, I wouldn't—"

"The problem is that I don't really know what you would or wouldn't do anymore. Since you've returned, I realize I really don't know you at all." She walked into the bathroom and slammed the door.

Dejected, Matt turned to the phone and figured he would use this time to call in his backup to meet up with them in DC.

Chapter 25

Indian summer entered with bright rays of sun shining down on DC. The men were finally together going over their part of the plan. "This is where I will go in with Mike, through the maintenance doors. We will enter as HVAC technicians, there to fix the AC unit. I won't even need bogus work orders. Peewee will stay in the van with Darrell." He turned to address Darrell. "Darrell, can you disable the unit nearest to Masters' office? That will get us up on his floor without any questions asked. Can you shut cameras off too?"

Matt now studied his comrade, Darrell, who smirked with a cocky attitude. "I can shut down the whole fucking floor if you want. The whole block!"

"Great." Matt continued, "The objective is for me, Kade, and Mike to get into his office or home, kill him, and destroy the files on his computer. You said you would have a computer in the van. All I'll have to do is turn his computer on and insert the flash drive."

"Right. Then I can remotely hook up to his computer and get into it bypassing any passwords. I'll have the newest communications devices for all of us to wear. Just listen for my voice and, once I tell you I'm in, you start the program I showed you on the drive. It will do all the work for you." He turned to address Kade too. "Just use the flash drives I gave you and Kade. Push the drive into the USB port. When you see the program just click on it when I say. It should take about thirty seconds to upload a virus that will destroy each computer's hard drive." Darrel talked about those flash drives as though he was their proud daddy.

Kade added to their conversation. "That's great. It will look like he was trying to hide something if both his office and home computers are destroyed. If you can, make sure to leave his prints on your flash drive. That way the authorities will think he used it on his office computer first, and then came home to use it on his home computer." This time Kade addressed Darrel. "Will any computer wizards be able to pull any information up from the destroyed hard drives?

"Not with the virus I created. Nothing will be found."

"Good. Peewee, you are driving the HVAC van. LL, you are driving the lawn service van. They mow his grass once a week, and I've coincided all of the plans with this. There won't be any vehicle at his home or office that hasn't been approved nor had an established pattern of being there. Of course, we will have the duplicated vans of the two service companies. Peewee knew a man who decals cars, and they're done and ready for us.

Domenica, you will wait in the landscaping van with LL." Kade instructed.

"No I won't. I'm going in with you."

All heads turned to Kade who slowly looked over at her.

"You are staying in the van, or you don't go. No arguments. We are trained in this sort of operation, and you are not. Do you want to be the reason for one of our deaths?"

She thought a moment before answering. "No, I don't." She looked at all of them. "I guess I'm staying in the van."

"Okay then. We observe both targets for another week to watch for any other patterns, especially of bodyguards or other security either in the building or with him, and then we go. Next Wednesday—lawn day."

Matt turned to Mike to review their part of the plan, "Mike, you and I will study the floor plans of the building for alternative escape routes. Then we will…"

Quietly, Kade walked up to Domenica and whispered in her ear. "Can you go for a walk with me a second?"

She studied him a moment and then nodded her head yes. He guided her out to the side of the motel where there was a quiet wooded area with a worn path. It was probably used by guests who had dogs to walk.

As they wandered away from the motel, Kade turned to her and said, "Domenica, I…I needed to tell you…what I mean is… Damn it! I love you! I know I told you that before, but just in case something goes wrong, I need you to know that. Tricking you wasn't part of the plan. I mean, it started out as part of the plan but… I don't want you to think…What I'm saying is what I feel for you is real and…"

The all-omnipotent Kade was grasping at words. This powerhouse, who commanded any room he walked into, was groveling like a peasant to his queen. Domenica roughly pulled him close and gently placed her lips on his. She swirled her tongue around his lips until he automatically opened his mouth to let her in, his tongue tangling with hers gently at first, but soon they became engulfed in a passion bottled for so long that it wanted to explode.

He positioned his hands under her ass and lifted her up. She automatically wrapped her legs around his waist as he backed her up against a large oak tree. His hand started to explore her body, sliding under her blouse and pushing her bra up until he was circling her nipple with his thumb as she softly moaned. She broke away from the kiss gasping for air. "Kade, I—"

"No! No more excuses. I might die, Domenica. I need you more than air. Christ, more than anything on earth. I need you. Please."

He demanded her lips; she gave them. She lowered her legs to the ground. His hands moved to the top of her blouse, and his fingers moved clumsily. Top button undone on her blouse, next button undone, third button undone.

She quickly unzipped his jeans and worked her hands into his boxers, grabbing and squeezing his dick as he groaned in pleasure. "Fuck yeah, baby."

"Domenica!" The call came from the motel parking lot area. "Domenica!" They both stopped and looked toward the motel. Matt was calling her. She placed her forehead against Kade's. They both sighed.

Then, she sadly gazed up into his eyes realizing what she had almost done. "We better get back, Kade."

"Domenica!" Matt's voice sounded out again.

"Fucking cock-blocker." Kade said under his breath. "He knows exactly what he is doing."

"Kade?" Her eyes connected with his as guilt overwhelmed her. "This was wrong of me to lead you on. I apologize. I should not put my own needs above anyone's."

"Baby, any time you want to put your needs first, I'm the man to use. I won't stop you. Go ahead and use me up." That lascivious smile was plastered across his face as he zipped back up.

She smiled at him while she buttoned up her blouse and pushed her fingers through her hair. "You always make me laugh, Kade." She nonchalantly dragged her fingers slowly across his arm. "I'm going back to the room."

"I think I'll wait here a few minutes. You know, until things settle down."

She started back, but turned. "Kade?"

"Yeah."

"Please don't die. I love you too. Ti amo, Kade." With that, she walked out of the wooded area to the room where Matt was waiting to talk to her.

Chapter 26

It was three o'clock in the afternoon—lawn day Wednesday. The HVAC van pulled up to the security checkpoint at the OGA building.

"We're here to check the AC unit for the fourteenth flour. Here are the work order papers signed by your maintenance supervisor." Peewee stated officially.

"Yes, we have the confirmation from our head of security." The guard briefly looked over the paperwork. "Man, I'm glad I don't work on that floor today, especially with all this heat. At least you guys got out here right away." He handed the papers back to Peewee.

"We should only need a few hours to fix the outside unit for that floor. But we have to check the vent work in the offices to make sure that's all working correctly."

The security guard directed them to the left. "Park over there after you unload your equipment."

The van drove into the lot, unloaded, and parked in the designated area.

"That was fucking easy," Mike snickered.

Matt and Mike entered the building with heads down and caps pulled to just above their brows. They passed another security station where guards also looked for their maintenance supervisor's signature that allowed the HVAC men to go ahead and continued to the elevators.

They both slipped on a pair of work gloves. Careful not to lift their faces to the security cameras, Matt carried on a bogus dialogue, "Listen, we should be able to fix that unit in a few hours. Then, we have to go to the one on Carter Street."

"Yeah. We should be able to pound out both jobs today." Mike answered.

They walked into the elevator and hit fourteen. It was a long few seconds up to their destiny. *Ding!* The doors opened.

Seated at a desk in front of the Colonel's office was a petite little blonde-haired beauty with a small fan blowing into her face. They walked over to her with papers in hand. "We're here to look over the AC unit vents. Judging by your fan, this is definitely the floor that is having the issues."

"Lord, yes," she responded as she took the papers and fluttered her eyes over them. "I'm practically melting up here." She smiled at Matt, but her flirtatious glances noticed Mike's stares as he perused her body from head to toe, stopping much longer than appropriate at her cleavage. "It kicks on every now and then, but not enough to keep it cool up here. Oh! Also, I noticed this all started yesterday morning."

Mike smiled as he took back the papers knowing that Darrell hacked into the building systems yesterday to cause issues. "I wish I could just leave like the Colonel did today. He told me to call him when you fixed it. Now he has the life. Golfing midmorning and then working from home in the afternoon—in the air conditioning."

"Well, we don't want a pretty little thing like you to melt. That would just be a shame," Mike stated with a flirtatious smile.

Matt decided the Colonel hired her more for her looks than for her ability. "I'm going to check the vents in the offices first. I'll need access to both rooms in this area."

He watched as she grabbed the keys from her desk and walked, with an obvious sway in her hips, to open the Colonel's office and the other door to a conference room before returning to her desk.

"Mike, check the one in here while I see if we are getting a cross vent from the other two rooms." As he said this, he made eyes at Mike while he subtly flipped his head toward her.

He probably could have told her that the ductwork had to be coordinated with the background music playing while the elevators went up and down, and she would have believed him. He walked into the Colonel's office as Mike turned to the flirtatious secretary.

"So how long have you been working for this company?" He leaned over her desk checking out her cleavage while blocking what was going on behind him in the Colonel's office. "I'm Justin, by the way, and you are?"

"Delilah. Delilah Murphy. I've been here about a year now." She giggled as she extended her dainty hand to him, which he promptly took and brought up to his lips to kiss. "My, my, aren't you the gentleman, gloves and all," she quipped giving him a once-over with her eyes.

Matt looked back to see Mike's ass and wide back hiding him from the secretary. He was keeping her busy by flirting with her while Matt turned the Colonel's computer on and waited until it was ready to go. He slipped the flash drive into the USB port. "So far, so good," he said so that Darrell could hear from his position in the van.

"Got it." Matt and Mike heard in their earpieces.

While Darrell hacked into the Colonel's computer, Matt went to the vents pretending to check them out, even unscrewing the vent cover and peering inside with his flashlight.

"So far, so good," he called again as Mike and Delilah turned around to see him working. Then from their earpieces, they heard Darrell say, "You're in."

Mike turned back to Delilah as Matt slipped back to the computer.

"So, if I asked for your number, could we set up a dinner date sometime?" He continued to mesmerize her. She scribbled down her number as Matt clicked on the program and opened it. It automatically started to download. Thirty seconds to go.

"I'm not getting a cross vent in here," Matt called out to Mike as he walked to the conference room. Mike didn't have to worry about blocking any view in that room so he turned back to Delilah with Matt in full view.

"While he's checking that room, let me check your area vent. I wouldn't want a beautiful woman like you to suffer in this heat. It would be such a shame." Delilah watched Mike as he took apart the vent, held a device up to it, and pretend to read the device. Then, he called out to Matt, "This vent is definitely working. Airflow is great."

Darrell listened to both of their chatter and responded to them through their earpieces. "If I didn't know any better, I would say you two are premiere HVAC technicians, especially you Mike with your electronic voltage tester that checks air flow instead of electrical voltage. But then again, what do I know?"

His next comment, he directed to Matt. "From what I can see here, the virus has been uploaded to the computer. You might want to go in and see if the folders you are looking for are gone. I had the virus destroy anything with the names Matt Hoover, Mike Cannon, or Kade Abraham or any combinations of those names in the files including the folder they were in. The computer should freeze in about two more minutes if everything works."

Matt started to put the vent together, and then packed up his tools to walk back to the Colonel's office.

"Next, you need to do a forced shut down and get the hell out of there. From what I'm seeing here, the folders you and Kade were in are no longer on his computer, but they are on mine. I downloaded the folders here onto my hard drive, so if something goes wrong with our ops, you have some blackmail material. Just. In. Case! Damn, I'm that good!"

Smiling, Matt walked to the Colonel's office giving Mike the eye. "So what about that dinner date, gorgeous?" he asked as he returned to the position in front of her.

Delilah looked up at him batting her lashes. "If you *do* call, I'll let you know then," she flirted back.

Matt could not see a few folders that at first were on the desktop. As he ejected the disk, the computer suddenly froze. Good. To. Go. He forced a shut down and said to Mike, "Okay. We got everything up here in order. Now let's go to that unit and install the new compressor.

"Nice talking to you Delilah." Mike slid his hand across hers.

"Bye, Justin." She smiled. "You too…

"Homer." Matt called back to her as he left the area.

"You too, Homer." Delilah was still waving as the elevator door closed.

***

While Matt destroyed the Colonel's computer, Kade was going through the private security checkpoint of the Colonel's gated community.

"Here to do some yard work," LL chimed to the guard.

"Go ahead through. With all this rain, I was expecting you guys a few days ago." The guard looked into the van.

"Naw. We cut when our clients call us. Our clients must not be able to afford two cuts in a week." LL said as he smiled.

Yeah, riiight," the guard answered back sarcastically. "Especially in *this* neighborhood."

LL pulled up to the house and backed into the driveway. When they reconned the Colonel's home, they found no cameras, only a security system that he apparently put on when he and his wife left the premises. Maybe he figured a gated community was all the protection he needed. Maybe he figured no one would dare come after him.

Domenica remained in the van with LL while Kade exited from the back of the van dressed for landscaping work. He slid on a pair of work gloves. He also had his cap pulled down over his eyes. He was just about to close the back door of the van and to sneak to the back of the house when he heard Domenica whisper to him. "*Ti amo*, Kade."

"*Ti amo*, Domenica." He turned to make his way to the back door.

In the meantime, LL had already unloaded the mower and started on the front yard. The noise could hide a gunshot if necessary. Today, it was necessary.

When Kade entered the back yard, he could not believe his luck. The Colonel had his back door open to draw in some fresh air. "LL. I need noise close to the house in case the screen squeaks when I open it." LL nonchalantly started to mow close to the windows of the house, which was his next area anyway since he had the area by the sidewalk finished.

Kade stealthily opened the back screen and entered making sure it did not slam behind him. Quietly, with gun drawn, he glided through the kitchen and into the adjacent hall. He peered into the first room off the hall. A dining room with no one in it. Just a few more rooms to go through.

Suddenly, a phone rang in the next room. Kade froze. "Colonel Masters here. Yes…So they fixed the AC? …Okay, but I'm still coming in tomorrow… I don't think I have to give you a reason since I'm the boss, and you are the secretary… If anyone asks just tell 'em I'm working from home…Yes. Goodbye." He slammed down the receiver. "What a fucking dumb bitch. It's a good thing God gave her a set of amazing tits." He went back to the porn site he was diligently watching.

Kade suddenly appeared in the doorway, gun drawn, startling the Colonel who automatically move to open his side drawer.

"Ah-ah-ah! I wouldn't move if I were you." Kade called out to him. "If you even breathe funny, I will blow your head off."

After the initial shock, Masters sat back in his chair staring at Kade. "Well, well, well. If it isn't Pussy-Whipped. Did you kill Hoover? Or do I have to put out a contract on you?"

"Oh, I think you already have one out on me. And no, Matt is not dead. A funny thing about Matt. I actually know him from the military. In fact, I saved his ass on a mission gone bad. We're good friends. I figured it wouldn't be right to save him one minute and kill him the next." Kade could see the anger boiling over in the Colonel's eyes.

"You fucking dick! You are dead, Kade! You are a motherfucking dead man walking!"

"Wow! Such bad language! The way I see it, you are the dead man if you don't do what I say. But first I need to destroy your computer." He handed the flash drive to the Colonel. "Put this in the USB port and no funny business." The Colonel took the drive from him and slid it into the port as Kade moved closer so the aimed gun was closer. "You are good at taking orders. Now start that program on it."

As Masters obeyed by starting the program, he asked, "What is this? I could just tell you what's on here before I—"

Instead of turning back to face Kade, he instantly reached on the other side of the computer grabbing his gun and aiming it at Kade. "Well, well, well. It looks like a stalemate. Put the gun down now, Kade."

"Not a fucking chance in hell." There was a brief moment of quiet while each waited for the other to flinch. Finally, Kade spoke. "I just need to know one thing. Why? Why did you start to kill innocent people?"

"I needed to show the government that our organization was the better one since they wanted to cut back on the program. Kade, you know we have enemies, you *know* we have to kill them. We're the only ones who can get rid of the garbage quickly. No years of trials, no millions of dollars in legal fees on both sides. Come on, man. Drop your gun and come back into the fold. All will be forgiven. You are our best. I don't want to lose you."

"Too late for that. I know you don't leave loose ends. I'm a loose end now. Drop your gun." Suddenly, Kade saw a shadow on the wall to the left of the Colonel. He instantly turned to shoot, as did the Colonel. "Domenica! What the Fuck?" Kade immediately turned the gun back to the Colonel.

Colonel Masters did not waste a second, his gun still pointed at her. "Well, well, well. If it isn't Wonder Pussy. Congratulations on turning my men into sniveling cowards." Without moving his gun from Domenica, he commanded, "Drop your gun, Kade, or I kill *her*." His smile was slyly vicious, knowing he would win this one.

Chapter 27

Kade stood motionless as he scrutinized Masters' gun pointing directly at the only woman he ever loved.

"Don't do it, Kade. He will kill us both." Domenica looked at him with pleading eyes.

"What's on the flash drive?" The Colonel directed his remark to Kade.

"It destroys everything on your computer. Just in case Matt and I are on there."

"Pretty smart. It must have worked. The computer froze up. You know I'm going to have to kill both of you. A spy crime gone bad. Fuck, I'll be a hero! Again!"

This time Domenica responded. "You can only kill one of us. Me! Kade will kill you."

He studied both of them a second and demonstrated a guttural laugh.

Suddenly, a maelstrom of events collided together in a millisecond of time.

In that millisecond, their actions occurred instinctively. The Colonel swung his gun back to Kade who had the only weapon to kill him. Domenica reacted to this by throwing herself in front of Kade while screaming, "Look out!" As he pushed her down with one hand. He aimed and shot with the other.

Silence.

Kade looked around to see the effects of the rat-a-tat-tat of events.

The Colonel's brains were splattered on the wall behind him; his eyes stared out into space.

Domenica lay at his feet, blood oozing from her.

"You guys alright?" Darrell's nervous voice brought Kade back to the reality of the moment over his earpiece.

Quickly, he was kneeling beside her. "Domenica? Oh God!"

"I'm okay, I think. Just hit on the arm." She used her other hand to put pressure on it as Kade went over every inch of her body. "Fuck! It hurts like a son of a bitch!"

"What the fuck were you thinking coming in here and flying across me?" Kade's worry turned to anger.

"I wanted to help you."

"Well, you almost got yourself—"

Again, Darrell's voice boomed over the earpieces. "I think we all can argue pretty when we finish the op. LL, if you're done with the yard, go in there and retrieve Wonder Pussy. Kade, do your thing in his office. Now! Clean up any of her blood."

LL responded. "I'm done with the front yard. The back is all landscaped in stones and rocks. On my way to get Wonder Body. At least I got manners, Darrell."

In a few seconds, LL joined them, lifting Domenica and helping her out of there to take her to the van. Kade remained and set up the scene to look like the Colonel shot himself between the eyes. He wiped down the gun and placed it into Masters' limp hand. Then, he wiped everything he thought either of the two could have touched. Her blood was apparently soaked into her shirt only.

"Darrell, did you get to copy any folders from his home computer?"

"No, why?"

"I know he has a contract out on me. I just wanted to find out who it was."

"Maybe it's in one of the folders I got from his office."

Kade looked somber. "I hope so. I really do." Kade turned to leave walking back to the van where LL had the mower packed up and ready to go.

"Glad this is over," LL said. "Let's get the fuck outta here."

When Kade jumped into the van, he went directly to Domenica evaluating her injury. LL already had bandages from the first aid box applied to her wound. It wasn't deep but she would need medical attention that a hospital could not supply. Jamal!

***

Both vans met at the pre-designated destination in the old warehouse district where they all loaded up into a third van. Peewee set the other two vans on fire with enough gasoline thrown inside and around them to make them burn down to nothing but metal.

Ops done and the devil destroyed, they headed back home.

"Kade?" Domenica reached out to him. He turned away. "Back there you were so worried, and now you're ignoring me?"

"Domenica, just leave me alone for a while. Please." He didn't want to ignore her now that she was injured but like all humans, he went into the what-could-have-happened scenarios. "I'm not mad at you, but I just have to get through this. Let me process all this please."

In a few minutes, Matt started to yell at her. "What the fuck were you thinking? You could have died! I told you to stay in the fucking van. We all agreed."

"Wrong! I did not agree." She looked like the devil himself staring at Matt. "I just thought I could help. You know, cover his back."

"I didn't need your help." Kade yelled now. "You could have died!" he reiterated.

"Please everyone stop yelling at me. I know I did wrong. Please stop yelling!" She started to cry. Both men moved to go to her, but Matt was closer. Matt pulled her into him holding her close.

"Shhhh, baby. I just don't know what I would have done if something happened to you. My life would have ended too."

Kade watched the two of them interact, and instantly he had a terrible epiphany. They belonged together. Matt loved her; she loved him. Their passion had its own life source. Fuck! He could almost see its aura. It took a hold of them when they were with each other. They fed off it. The life source connected their hearts, their dreams, and their future. Kade would never have that with her. Never! He realized that now. She. Would. Never. Be. His.

He should be happy that he had some time with her. However, it was not even close to enough time. He would have to leave. He could not stay around her and not have her. That torture was too much to bear. He suffered through an entire war zone, but this would kill him. Seeing her by the side of another man, a man he considered a brother in arms. How could anyone live with that?

"Kade, are you okay?" Domenica still looked for forgiveness.

"Yeah. Just peachy." Kade moved to the back of the van, as far away from her as he could. Now, his life's painting would go back to just black and white. No bright spot of color anywhere, anymore.

Chapter 28

"Hold still. I need to put this antiseptic on it." Jamal dabbed her wound, then covered it with white gauze.

"Ow, ow, ow!" she cried out.

"You are such a fucking baby!"

After he said that to her, she gave him a dirty look. "You try getting shot and see how it feels. I had to lie and tell the coach I fell on broken glass when I was home and cut it. So I'm out of diving for a few more weeks."

"It's a good thing it's the middle of October. You should be good to go in a few weeks." Then he added as an afterthought. "I just want to know something. How many more of your friends and you am I going to have to patch up? You know what I am doing is illegal."

"I know, and I appreciate it more than you could ever know." She looked at him and smiled. "Pretty sure this is the last one."

"Pretty sure?" he called out to her as he exited her apartment.

She stood and went to her phone. She dialed Kade a few times earlier that morning, but there was no answer. *Maybe he has real-estate work to tend to*, she thought. It rang and rang going to voicemail again. "Kade. What the fuck?

Answer your phone already. Please don't be angry." She hung up and decided to face him.

How long could he remain angry, for God sake? She ran up the flights of stairs to his room and pounded on the door. No answer. She pounded again. "I know you're in there, Kade. I hear movement. Please let me in."

She heard steps toward the door and thought, *Finally*. An older woman answered the door. She was in the building's cleaning uniform propping a mop by her side. "Mr. Abraham is not here."

"Oh. Then I'll come back later."

"No. He's gone. He's in Florida."

"What do you mean he's in Florida?" Domenica brushed pass the woman and ran into his apartment looking around. No sign of him and more importantly, no smell of him. "Kade?" She ran to the bedroom and stared at the open closet. Most of his clothes were gone. Just a few garments hung in the vast closet, looking as though their owner had abandoned them. She ran back to the house cleaner. "Florida?"

"The only thing I know is I am to dust this apartment every week for the next six months or even longer."

"What?" Domenica felt her legs wobble as she quickly sat on his couch. *He left? He didn't tell me he was going. Was my action really so serious that he ended our friendship without a word?* Tears started to well in her eyes. "I can't…I can't believe this." She did not even know how to feel. She was not exactly his girlfriend, but she thought he at least would have said goodbye to her. She didn't know how to get in touch with him if he didn't answer his phone. Then she knew what to do. Matt.

She rushed back to her apartment and dialed. "Yeah." Matt sounded as though he was napping.

"Kade is gone. Do you know where he went?"

Matt remained quiet for a while. He then answered sarcastically. "Domenica. Hi. I'm fine. And you? How are you feeling?"

"I am fine. Do you know what happened to Kade?" she repeated.

"Um, no." He paused wondering why she was so worried about where Kade was. "I can tell you this. If Kade wants to stay hidden, he can and will." There was a long silence before he continued. "Listen, Domenica, can we go out somewhere and talk?" He hated this part about loving her: the uncertainty of their love, the despair of knowing there might be another. She held all the cards in a game he had no experience in playing. A game he was losing.

"About what, Matt? How you only came back to see if I was fucking someone? Or how about when you tell me to do something that I had better do it."

"Yes. About that and other things. Domenica, please don't shut me out. The danger is gone. We can finally be together. Okay?" He waited for her answer.

She realized she had to face each man, one at a time. She could not leave either of them in limbo anymore—not as they'd left her. "Yes. Do you want to go to dinner?"

"That's fine. How about five?"

"See you then at The Library." She still was going to keep it safe and distant until both of them discussed their situation, to see if they even could try again.

This was the time where both Matt and she made it or ended it. The romantic phase, where the lovers saw each other as perfect, was apparently over. In that phase, a person could only try to be perfect to the other for so long, and then the true self emerged—all the imperfections, the ugly along with the good. If the two of them could survive each other's faults, then they were meant for each other.

She was just not sure anymore. Matt was starting to display traits that she could not live with. Jealousy and control.

Every woman who ever read a romance novel fell in love with that alpha male, the one who came in and swept the heroine off her feet. Who wouldn't? He lived by his own code, he loved passionately, he followed his own path—an independent loner in a society of mostly conformists. However, Domenica knew that in real life, although these two alpha men of hers were truly amazing, they had that personality that clashed with hers.

If Matt could adjust to her need for independence, if he could live with her talking to and associating with the other gender of her species, if he could love her faults as well as her good qualities, maybe then, all would be right again.

After all, she was an alpha too. She knew this. It didn't take much to realize she was not like most of the other women, the yes-dear ones. Not that there was anything wrong with those women. She was just not like that. She knew that sex was not the only thing that was important in a marriage; a couple needed respect for and dedication to each other.

And yet, though she needed independence to explore her career and dreams, let's face it, no one woke up cuddled against a career and dreams in the middle of the night.

She plopped on the couch and dialed her mom.

"What's wrong?" Her mother knew her like the lyrics to her favorite song.

"Just guy problems? Why does finding the right one have to be so difficult?" She just dove right into the problem.

"I ask that all the time," her mother answered.

"What?" Domenica could not hide her shock.

Her mother was silent a moment and then began. "It doesn't end with finding the right one. That's just the beginning. That's when the hard work really starts. Every day forever until one of you dies. It's hard work. To be in a relationship. To be married." Domenica let her continue. "It is a constant struggle every day, because you want one thing, and he wants another, and the battle never ends."

"Then how did you and Dad stay married for so long?"

Her mother must have been contemplating the answer. "I am going to use a very non-romantic word. You might find it very boring. Reciprocation."

"What the hell, Mom."

"Hear me out." Her mother continued. "It's not about if he gives you your way all the time or you give him his way. It's about if you do something for him, he does something else for you. It's about no one feeling short-changed. I really think it is as simple as that."

"Short-changed, huh."

"Yep. I have to wash the dishes tonight, but he has to dry them. Or I have to take the kids to practice, but he will pick them up. He has to go shopping with me, but I have to sit and watch a football game with him. It's about no one feeling like they were taken advantage of, you know, for granted."

"So that's how it worked in your marriage?"

"Hell no!"

Both laughed at her exclamation.

"Hopefully, you get the picture." As the laughter faded, she continued, "Oh, I adjusted. All women try to adjust. Most don't and divorce. I just knew I had responsibilities to children first and then to Dad." She went on. "It wasn't all bad. There were plenty of good times. But bearing the burden by yourself is so difficult. It should have involved two. Should always involve two—on everything. Thank God he reciprocated on many other occasions."

"So you found happiness?"

"Whoa, Domenica. You do not *find* happiness. You create it." Her mother was silent a few moments probably trying to figure out how she could explain a lesson that age taught her. "You create happiness today and then live in it as long as it allows you. It is not something you can capture and keep, because tomorrow happiness might escape your grasp." She was quiet again probably reflecting on other incidents in her own life. "Happiness promises nothing. It doesn't visit you; you visit it. The sooner you learn that, the easier your life becomes."

"Well, I can see I caught you in a philosophical mood today." Domenica sighed.

I guess so." Her mother began again. "Listen Domenica, before I go, I will leave you with one last bit of advice. Never regret whatever it was that carried happiness with it into your life.

Domenica replied, "I will take your advice, Mom. But I will add that you have to be very wary of what that *whatever* is." Domenica thought of Matt and Kade.

"True. People are so starved for happiness that they accept things like alcohol, drugs, or even the wrong person to love just to fill that need. Listen, I really have to go. Yoga class—one of my whatevers. Bye, Domenica. Love you more. Oh, and watch out for the *whatevers* in your life."

"Bye Mom. I will." She hung up the phone, started toward her bedroom, and uttered under her breath, "Whatever."

Chapter 29

Kade listened to the birds sing to the sun as he left his office. He still resided in Atlanta, but just tweaked his schedule so he would not run into Domenica anywhere. Just like recovering alcoholics could not associate with other alcoholics or hang out in bars, he could not attempt to see her.

She was his drug of choice, and he had to drain her out of his system—cold turkey. He did not answer her calls. He did not visit her on campus, since she was now back on campus. He did not even go to the same familiar places he took her. He couldn't. The old places produced images of her. The pain it created was a sharp knife plunging into his heart.

He would survive Domenica. He had survived bullets whizzing by him in a military hot spot, for Chrissake! He just needed to continue to extract every essence of her out of his being.

That meant going to his office early in the morning to do paper work or late at night when she was working. He could call in instructions to his workers during the day if needed. The new restaurants were always places he wanted to check out anyway. So now, that's what he was doing.

He was staying in one of his other apartment buildings he had planned to renovate. Now, with him living there, he could participate in all the construction. This one would even be better than his old apartment.

Hell, I even switched to another gym. I can do this. I can remove her from my brain, wipe the slate clean, erase her as if she never existed.

"Who the fuck am I trying to kid?" he verbalized aloud.

It had been over a month, and he still woke up thinking about her. Christ, he fell asleep thinking about her. Whoever said it was better to love and lose was a fucking dumb asshole!

Kade mentally kept busy. He accomplished more work in those four weeks than he did all year. Everything in his office and his new home office was organized and completed. In fact, all he did was work. That kept her images at bay. His forced thoughts on work circulating in his mind kept him on point. *Stay on the phone. Stay buried in work. Buy and sell new real estate. Make money, make money, make money.*

He needed to stay focused. If he was thinking of her, he would not be thinking of a possible assassin sent to kill him. He had to concentrate on that. *Make money, make money. Watch for signs of an intruder. Focus, focus.*

Although at night? Yeah. That's when fucking D-Day happened in his brain.

She crept into his dreams—a place where he could not put up barriers—like a conspiring assailant. There, she pulled out all the drawers of stored memories that treacherously edge themselves into his brain. Him kissing her, feeling her, holding her, comforting her, and laughing with her. Memories that ultimately produced that wonderful high in his soul that he was trying to fight.

Then, these memories would be projected over and over again on this big movie screen in his mind. There, he could not miss seeing all, feeling all, and hearing all. Abruptly, he would shoot up from his sleep, sweating profusely and swearing belligerently, because suddenly she was gone. He didn't want her to be gone. In a millisecond, he hated whatever it was that woke him up. An alarm clock, thunder from a storm, even having to piss which was a normal bodily function! Anything that took him away from his nightly euphoria. Fuck!

The beauty in the dreams of her always morphed into the ugly in the realities of him.

***

He pushed back from his desk, stood, and walked to the window in his office. He turned to look at the clock. Another late night, after midnight. It was so dark outside even with the streetlight in the middle of his block. He wiped his hand across his face and collected his papers placing them in his briefcase. Like every other night, his plan was to work on more projects at his new place until he was so exhausted he would eventually fall asleep.

He grabbed the office keys and headed for the door. His mind drifted to her. *I wonder if she works tonight. She'll be getting out of there soon. It doesn't matter. I won't go near the place anyway.* He walked out the door and locked it. *I have to stop thinking about her. Maybe if I find an easy lay for the night.* He went to unlocked his car, but with his hands full, he dropped the keys. He bent to retrieve them.

Bang! Bang!

Shots sliced through the air.

Kade dropped to the ground alongside his car. "Fuck! I'm hit." He grabbed at the upper right side of his arm with one hand, while retrieving his ankle gun with the hand of his injured arm. Stealthily, he crawled around to the other side of the car and listened. He pulled out his belt and wrapped it tightly around his upper arm to control the bleeding.

Bang! Another shot.

Now, he was glad he was in a dark area so the gunman could not see his movement. He would not shoot back—yet. Let the man think he killed him. He switched the gun to his good hand.

Think! Think! He appraised the situation as he looked around. The keys were on the ground on the other side of the car, so he couldn't drive away. Maybe he should make a run for it. The shots were coming from across the street between those two buildings. He still had his holstered gun under his jacket.

There appeared to be only one gunman. *Christ, it must be a new man, because I wouldn't have missed if it were my contract. Good to know. Experience is on my side.*

Bang! That one ricocheted off one of the garbage cans near him.

Kade laid low playing dead. *Let the fucker come to me.*

Bang!

Kade waited—his gun cocked and ready.

Suddenly, he saw a shadow move from between the two buildings. The man was craftily moving toward him to see if he could now collect the rest of his money.

Kade had to remain still, just a few minutes longer.

First, the man ran to the telephone pole with two garbage cans leaning up against it. He crouched between them.

Kade remained still.

He noticed the man's lowered arm between the space where the two cans tilted together. Not Kade's kill shot yet. In an instant, the man jumped up rushing to the bus stop enclosure, the sides made from treated lumber. There, Kade could only see his feet behind it. Still not a good shot.

He waited as the gunman started toward the other side of the car opposite Kade.

He pulled from all the experience he had from the military and from working at the OGA. He had to muster all his strength to shoot the man in his leg and then run around and shoot the kill shot. If he couldn't make it, he would be the dead one.

Just as he envisioned it, the man ran to the other side of his car where from underneath the car, Kade aimed at his lower calf and blew out the man's leg.

The man screamed, as he grabbed at his lower calf while crashing to the ground. "Aaaaaah!"

In no time, Kade was on his feet and around the car where he aimed at the man's head and pulled the trigger.

Bang!

Dead.

Still aiming at the man, Kade kicked the body to make sure he was dead. Then he slumped to the ground and felt for a pulse. Nothing.

Chapter 30

Pulling out his phone, he perused the area while the call connected. "Hey, I need a clean-up over here at my office."

"Kade? Haven't heard from you in a long time!"

"Yeah, well I've been undercover."

"I heard you wanted out."

"I just couldn't pass up the money on this one."

"Who is it this time? Drug affiliated? It's bad in this area."

"How soon?" Kade asked abruptly.

"Probably fifteen."

"Okay, make it quick, please." After disconnecting, Kade picked up his keys and briefcase, opened the car and sat in it waiting. He knew that no one could have imagined that he and Matt were the ones who wiped out Masters, so everyone was continuing their *usual* services. Moments later, he saw the familiar car and waved to it.

The man coming out of the car went to Kade, observing the scene. "Fuck. He shot you?"

"Yep. Guess I'm getting too old for this line of work. I better retire." He laughed as the man shook his head. "Can you take it from here?"

"You need help getting to a hospital? My guys here can get this cleaned up." The man was still in disbelief that someone had shot Kade Abraham. "Christ! It's a good thing your office is on this dead side street."

"Yeah, nobody bothers anyone or anything after five o'clock over here. Thanks, but I got this." Kade started his car and took off. It was good to know people who knew people in this business.

He drove around for a few minutes mindful that he could not go to his place. Masters would not have only sent that inexperienced kid to kill him. There had to be another gunman, one for him *and* Matt. Fuck. He didn't even know where Matt was staying. He kept driving until he knew no one was following him. He had to find a place where he could get help.

Domenica.

***

Domenica was happy because The Library was not busy tonight, so John let her leave early. She had just washed the grease and dirt off her body watching it swirl into the drain when she heard the doorbell ring.

"Hmmm. Nikki's at Dante's. Maybe Shannon decided not to stay over her other friend's apartment tonight. That will be a story I want to hear." She quickly put a towel around her and went to open the door.

"Did you two have a fight or—" She froze. "Kade."

"Domenica, I have to come in. I—"

"Oh, now you come back after all this time, ignoring my calls?" He swayed toward her. "What the fuck is wrong with you. Are you drunk? I'm not putting up with—"

She did not finish her rampage, because Kade stepped into her apartment and collapsed into her. She barely caught him in enough time so that he did not slam into the floor.

"Kade!" she screamed out as she guided him down to the floor, her hands now full of his blood.

***

"Domenica, seriously, I can't keep stitching up your friends." Jamal was triaging Kade this time. It was evident that he was serious about being the one, once again, to 'service' her friends who kept getting shot. Kade lay on the couch helplessly observing the two of them as they undressed him, then treated his wounded arm.

"Jamal, I'm sorry. I didn't know what else to do. It's kind of the same situation as Matt. He can't go to a hospital." Domenica was adjusting her t-shirt and sweats around her, since she threw them on in a millisecond before letting Jamal into her apartment.

Kade spoke up. "Jamal, you have to help Domenica drag me into that large storage area behind that armoire. Domenica, I killed Masters' agent tonight, but I don't know if there is one more after me. I'm sure no one followed me, but he might come here on his own to see if I'm staying at your place. If he even knows about you. If he finds me here with you, we are both dead." Rambling on and on, Kade's brain prioritized more instructions to Domenica and Jamal. "If you can get in touch with Matt, tell him I think the last guy is after both of us. He has to be careful too. He *has* to protect you."

With lips pressed together, Jamal just shook his head quite disgusted with the situation. He finished bandaging Kade, "I know you work the same place Matt does." He could tell Kade was weak from some loss of blood, but probably more so from shock. The wound was not serious enough for him to have to rush Kade to a hospital.

"Nope. Matt and I presented our permanent resignation to Colonel Masters quite a few weeks ago. But I *did* work there" No matter how weak he was, Kade still came up with those flippant remarks. Domenica just rolled her eyes at Kade.

"Come on, Domenica. Help me get him to this closet. Where is it?"

"Right there, behind the armoire. Just slide the pocket door open after I push this out of the way." With the furniture coasters underneath it, she easily slid the armoire away from the pocket door to the closet. "Wait. Let me get the air mattress ready for him."

She went into the hidden storage room, pulled out the air mattress, and filled it. In no time, the mattress was prepared and pushed back into the storage closet. She searched for extra sheets and blankets, throwing them on the mattress. Carefully, they both led Kade to the mattress, lowering him down on it. Jamal hastily walked out of the closet and back toward her apartment door.

"Jamal?" Domenica followed him to the door. "I'm so sorry."

"Yeah, I know. You're always sorry. Just keep the wound clean and make sure he takes the antibiotics so it don't become infected. Pain pills when he needs 'em." He turned to walk out but faced her again. "Don't call me for anything like this again. Understand?"

"Yes." She answered somberly. She knew he meant it.

She closed the door as he walked away without looking back. Then she rushed to Kade. She wiped the sweat from his face with a cool, wet washcloth. She raised his head up and helped him drink water to wash down the pain pill. She helped him back down, covered him, and stood up to leave.

"Domenica?" he called out weakly.

"Yes, Kade?"

"Go get my gun by my clothes and put it on the floor by me, just in case. If any situation arises, don't be afraid to use it. I'll be too drugged up to save you. Can you do it?"

"Yes. If the situation arises." She answered as she retrieved the gun.

"And Domenica? Please don't leave me alone." His panicked eyes stared into hers.

This was not the man she knew, the monolith of unyielding purpose, a man who was in control of his life, who demanded respect, who feared nothing. She pursed her lips together as she witnessed a frightened child-like being lying down in front of her. The uncharacteristic sight of him wrenched at her heart. Instantly, she walked back to Kade, slid in behind him, and covered both of them. "Just relax," she said. "I got this." She nestled in closer, placing her arm around his waist, as she checked out her excellent view of where the gun was in regards to the apartment door. A straight shot—just in case.

She held him tight, being careful of his wound, as he whispered, "Thanks Domenica. I love you." With that, he fell into a deep sleep, never noticing the few tears escaping down Domenica's cheek.

Chapter 31

The next morning as Domenica was preparing breakfast, she jumped when she heard the keys in the door lock. Shannon or Nikki was home. She would have to tell them both. There was no way she could hide a six-foot something man in that closet without them knowing. She picked the gun up anyway, walking to the door with it as it opened and then closed. She looked into Shannon's bright eyes.

"God, me and Marianne worked on our communications project until three this morning. I swear I fell asleep on a piece of pizza. Whoa!" Shannon yelled out as soon as she spotted the gun. Domenica quickly placed it on the nearby table as Shannon pushed through the door and closed it. "What's with the gun? Who's that sleeping in our storage closet?" For being the artsy type always in her own world, Shannon never missed anything.

"Wow. You get right to the point." Domenica scratched her bed head. "Shannon. Sit down. I need to tell you something. Something that might get you killed."

Shannon fell back into the plush couch. "Yeah, right." She laughed at Domenica's remark. "If I tell you, I'll have to kill you, right?" Her eyes quickly returned to the gun positioned on the side table next to her.

"No. This is serious. I'm not joking." Domenica proceeded to tell her about Matt and Kade and their jobs. In fact, she explained all that recently transpired—except for them killing Masters—while Shannon's eyes popped open in wide amazement. "He was shot early this morning by another gunman, and he wants to hide out here until this gets resolved. I can't make this decision alone since you and Nikki live here too, so what do you say? If you tell me he has to go, he goes. No hurt feelings."

Shannon still appeared to be in a state of utter shock looking back and forth from the sleeping Kade to Domenica. She finally asked, "Is he certain no one followed him here?"

"Yeah. Pretty sure. We would have had a visitor already if he was followed."

"And it's just for a few days?"

"Yes. Maybe a week at the most."

"I guess it's okay. But I don't know what Nikki will say." Shannon looked back at Kade. "Holy shit." Her brain started to process all of this information.

Domenica gave her the biggest hug, and then she went into their kitchen to finish Kade's breakfast. Hopefully, he would wake up from the powerful pain pills Jamal gave him as soon as she had everything done. She walked back to the closet noticing that Shannon was staring at him.

"He *is* beautiful, isn't he?" Shannon remarked studying the sleeping Kade.

"Yes he is," Domenica answered, checking out his half-covered, semi-naked body with cut muscles in all the right places.

"It's kind of like when God was dishing out beauty dust, He was suddenly distracted by something—maybe Eve yelling at Adam to put his shit away. And then, when God refocused on Kade, He forgot He'd already sprinkled him, accidentally sprinkling a few more cups of beauty dust on him." Shannon was so sincere in her verbal abstraction, still studying Kade as though he were a work of art and she was interpreting what she saw.

Domenica had to smile at her. Domenica glanced back at the sleeping Kade. *God sprinkled more than a few more cups of beauty dust!* Appreciatively, they both took in the beautiful work of this living art form in front of them.

Suddenly, Shannon was pulled into the present. "Well, I'm going to my room to sleep since I didn't get much sleep last night." She picked up her book bag and headed to her room. "Night, Domenica. Try to keep the gunfights down to a minimum. If you need some muscle, just yell out."

"Night, Shannon." She smiled as she went back into the kitchen to plate and tray the food. She poured a cup of coffee for him and headed back into the storage closet. "Kade," she called softly. "Kade!" This time a bit louder.

"Huh, wha'?" Kade jumped up, but the pain from his injury caused his body to jerk back down to the bed. "Fuck! Where am? Domenica?" Confused, he slowly inspected his small room.

"You haven't come out of the closet yet." Domenica laughed at that. "I always wondered about you."

"No shit." Kade was wide-awake now remembering how he landed in this storage room. "Come over here and lay by me so I can get my hands on you, and I'll show you just how in-the-closet I'm not." He looked at her with lustful eyes, his morning woody lifting the sheet covering his lower half.

"Wow! Aren't we feisty this morning? So being shot also makes men horny?"

"Everything makes men horny, Domenica," He replied trying to sit up.

"I made you breakfast." With that, Domenica sat down beside him. "Here open your mouth." She silently fed Kade, switching from food to a swig of coffee, until all of it was gone.

Kade stared at her face all the while she fed him. After he could eat no more, he stretched and tried to get up again.

"Do you think you should try to stand?"

"If I don't use your bathroom, I'm going to piss myself," Kade remarked. "What the fuck kind of pain pill did Jamal give me? I'm still light-headed."

Jumping up to help him, Domenica reached out her hand to pull him up. She steadied him while he adjusted to the upright position and walked with him to the bathroom. "I am not holding anything else while you are in there. You are on your own with this, Kade."

His laughter filled the room. "Are you sure you don't want to help me? I am soooo weak I surely can't hold it up. And with all of its excess weight, you know, cuz my dick is so big."

"Um. No!" She stated this emphatically.

He finished and cleaned up for the day as best he could before he headed back to her. She walked him back to the air mattress where he fell into it exhausted. "Fuck! I feel like I hit into a brick wall. Those pills are worse than my injury!"

As he settled back, reality hit him. Quickly, he started to spew out all of his thoughts. "Listen, Domenica, you and the girls have to be careful. You can't answer the door without figuring who is on the other side. You have to watch to see if someone is following you. Check your car to see if anyone is inside. Better yet, keep it locked. I don't think they will come after you, but you have to be careful. I also think you should—"

"Kade. Kade!" He stopped talking for a moment. "We know how to be careful. We are single girls on a campus. What I need you to do is rest and get better." She sat on the floor beside him and started to brush his black hair out of his eyes. He grabbed her hand and gently kissed it.

"I am so sorry, Domenica. I tried to stay away from you. I didn't want to bring this to your doorstep again, but this was the only place I could go."

She just shook her head yes, as she checked his wound, cleaned it, and changed the bandage. "Jamal said that we only have to watch for infection, but he also has you on an antibiotic." Then she brought him a toothbrush and a cup of water.

After he was done with everything, he started to give her instructions, "You need to call Lima Bean and warn him. Also, have him pick up my car. I left it on Third and Liberty Street and walked the two miles here. He can park it at one of my offices, but take the keys. I'll leave a message for my employees that I'm out of town." He looked outside the door as he talked, trying to think of other things that had to be done. Suddenly his thoughts did a one eighty. "Is that a stripper's pole by that wall?" he asked astonished.

"Wow! ADHD at work here. Yes, I had one installed right in the dance area you made for me. I wondered how long it would take you to discover it."

"So you finally decided what your fucking major is, and it's stripping?"

Domenica laughed. "You wish! Strippers are not the only people who use those." She took his toothbrush, paste, and water to return them to the bathroom. "Eric and I practice our routines in here, and I figured since it's such a great work out, I would put one up. This way I can incorporate stretching, gymnastics moves, and dance moves into my work outs and into my time frame."

"Huh! I like the way you think. Show me some shit." All of a sudden, his mind forgot about a possible assassin who might be after him and the pain of his injury.

Domenica's brows furrowed together. "Um! Nooooo!"

"Come on! A dying man's last request."

"Not even if you *were* a dying man. Change the subject."

Kade looked back and forth between the pole and her.

"And stop fantasizing about me on the pole, Kade!" she ordered angrily, walking back into the bathroom hoping his one-track mind would soon forget about the pole. "Listen, I'm going to pick you up some t-shirts and sweats at the store. Anything else you might need?"

"Condoms? Maybe? Hopefully?"

Domenica came back just staring at him. "At least I know your near-death experience didn't change you any."

Suddenly, they both heard the door opening. Domenica rushed for the gun and aimed.

Nikki.

"Um…Why is Kade in our storage closet half dressed—not that I'm complaining—and more important, why are you pointing a gun at me? I mean, I like kinky, but even this is a bit over the top."

As she slammed the door shut, Domenica grabbed Nikki's arm and led her to the tell-all couch. How many times would she have to tell her story? Today, she felt like Ricky 'splainin' things to Lucy.

Chapter 32

Six days had passed and the start of the second week of November brought light flakes of snow, not enough to cover the ground but enough to let everyone know it was cold outside, colder than normal. To Kade's knowledge, no one was snooping around trying to find him. He was moving on his own without wincing in pain. He only took the pain pills at night so he could be clearheaded during the day. He also initiated a mild exercise routine so that he would not lose too much of his strength. Besides the t-shirts and sweats, he also had Domenica buy him a burner phone to keep in constant contact with Matt. "Did you see anything yet?"

Matt answered, "No. I've done surveillance around your main office and around your apartment. No one yet. Are you sure there's another one after us?"

"I'm not sure of anything with that fucking bastard Masters. I just don't want any surprises. Did you have any trouble accessing the camera footage to this place?"

"No, but it is almost impossible for one man to watch three places."

"Yeah, I know. Do the best you can. Maybe just spend most of your time watching this building. I don't want anything to happen to Domenica or the girls."

Matt was silent with Kade's last statement. Domenica apparently became the elephant in the room. "Put Domenica on for a moment."

Kade handed her the phone.

"Matt? You're okay?"

"Yes. Just trying to make sure nothing happens to you—or Kade. How you holding up?"

"Good. Kade is pretty much doing everything on his own. The girls and I are following our regular routine, and everything seems to be normal. It is just a situation that's really scary."

Matt wished he were there to comfort her. "I know, Domenica, I know. Listen, I gotta go. Remember I love you."

"Love you too." She hung up and handed the phone back to Kade, who was listening in on the conversation.

She hated how both of them were handling her as though she were this piece of delicate glass that could shatter at any time. Both were afraid, but not of the possible assassin. They were afraid she would choose the other one. In the apartment, she was subject to Kade's love stares. Outside the apartment, she was subject to Matt's combat-assassin-protector-badass mode staking out her building, and his incessant calling.

The great thing was she knew he could not come up to her apartment without creating a dangerous situation for the girls and Kade. The bad thing was that he was jealous enough to keep calling at all hours to see how Kade and she were doing. Translation: Is Kade cozying up to you? Better translation: Is Kade fucking you? His jealousy irritated Domenica to no end.

She was hoping she could start to experience muscle memory with Matt. All athletes knew what that was. In diving, her body reproduced movement without thinking about it all the time, even when she was away from it for a while. She hoped her heart could do this now. Could her heart pull up the love she had for him before? Before he left. Before he almost destroyed her.

***

Throughout the days, the girls kept the pocket door open with the armoire slid into place in front of it. If anyone broke into the place while the girls were on campus or at practice, they would never find Kade.

He spent his days chilling during that time on the mattress with Shannon's laptop. This device kept Kade busy for hours with his work. Today, as he worked on invoices, he heard the door click open.

No one should be coming in at this time. He was instantly on the defensive.

He grabbed the gun that was always on the floor by him. Slowly standing up, he quietly walked to the open doorway aiming his ear to where the edge of the armoire met the doorframe. He heard keys jingling, and a sigh of relief escaped from him. One of the girls was home actually quite early. Maybe a professor cancelled her class. He sat back down on his mattress and continued his work. Whichever one it was, she was trying to be quiet, because they all knew he took power naps in the afternoon.

About fifteen minutes later, he heard a strange thumping and swooshing sound on the other side of the door. He tried to ignore it, but after about ten more minutes of the thumping and swooshing, curiosity conquered his work ethic. He went to the door again. As quietly as he could, he gently pressed on the armoire, the furniture sliders making it a cinch to push it away from the doorway.

When he saw what was making the noise, he literally thought his heart would explode out of his chest. There in front of him, in the dance area he put in, Domenica was on the pole working out. She had just finished a movement, dismounted, and was again climbing up onto the pole.

Her cell phone was in the waist band of her leggings, and in her ears were the wireless earbuds he had bought her for Christmas. He smiled when he remembered telling her that with the ear buds, she would not bother her roommates or even her neighbors. When she bestowed upon him the biggest hug and kiss, he wanted to rush out and buy her fifty more. It was the best and worst kiss of his life, because there was only the one. Probably the first and last one from her now.

She was definitely lost in the music, because she didn't even notice he was watching her as he leaned against the doorframe. She had a black sports bra on, trimmed in shiny gold that pushed her tits in and up. Fuck! What he wanted to do to those tits!

Her bottoms looked like those little boy-shorts that the girls wear, the ones where their cheeks peek out at the bottom, only this one matched her top. And yes, her cheeks were definitely peeking out. The outfit was black shiny Lycra, hugging every curve on that woman's perfect body. Fuck! His dick was already hard, tenting through his sweats.

First, his heart stopped and now his breath choked off as she started her movement. Her muscular endurance was evident as she climbed up and wrapped around the pole. Then she pushed her body out holding it parallel to the ground with just the power in her arms, a human flagpole. Her hands encircled the pole, her legs went into a complete split. From this movement, she maneuvered into a revolving move where, as her bent leg clung around the pole, her whole body slowly and sensually swirled around it through the movement of just that leg. How the fuck did she accomplish that? From this, she then climbed up to the top and swung her other leg around holding on just by that leg. She slowly turned upside-down into a body inversion.

Suddenly, Domenica loosened her leg allowing her to drop to the floor, her head stopping inches above the floor. Her leg had tightened around the pole again to stop her body's quick downward fall.

Kade's body jerked to rush to her thinking she fell. When he realized it was one of her moves, he stood there paralyzed watching the fluidity of her movements. Art in motion.

Now, he at least knew what that swooshing sound was. It was the friction of her skin against the pole as she controlled the downward falls. Out here, it actually made a squeaky sound. She truly was art in motion, her body the artist, the pole her canvas, and her movements the medium.

Her core and upper body strength amazed Kade. He knew one thing: she would be the death of him. He couldn't live with her. He couldn't live without her. He was fucked big time because, like that song said, he couldn't make her fall in love with him. If it's not there, it's not there. No praying, wishing, hoping, longing, dreaming, lusting, desiring, crawling, or begging makes it happen, if it doesn't happen naturally.

He was truly fucked.

As she continued her arousing performance, he was drawn back to her body movement; his eyes hazed and darkened watching her. His dick was so hard it was actually painful. He envisioned her performing on top of him in his bed, stretching her legs out in a split while she was on top of him riding his own pole, his hands around her hips guiding her up and down. He was entranced. Fuck, he would have blue balls over this.

Suddenly, she dismounted and grabbed a towel to wipe off her sweat. She turned and abruptly stopped, finally seeing him standing there staring at her in his evidently aroused state. He couldn't even hide his erection if he wanted to, not through the sweat pants he donned.

She pulled the buds from her ears. "Not very nice to gawk at me, Kade," she stated sounding pissed. "Hope you enjoyed it."

Chapter 33

She started for the bathroom, but in two steps Kade was in front of her grabbing onto her arms and pushing her back against the mirrored wall. In a state of shock, she faced him. "Kade, what are you doing?" He was so close to her face, she could hear his breath rasping, could see his aggressive demeanor, his hooded eyes.

"Something I should have done a long time ago. Take control." His lips forcefully took over hers. His arms cocooned around her. His body slowly moved into hers.

Domenica started to push away. "Kade, don't," she moaned in a low, sultry voice as his rough hands grasped her waist jerking her in tighter against his body. His hands slipped to her firm ass, and he instantly lifted her up and pushed her against the mirrored wall for leverage. As his hardened dick ground into her, her legs innately straddled his waist. When his lips conquered hers, she parted her lips giving him permission to invade with his tongue.

Her fingers tangled in his soft black hair when she lustfully returned his kisses. "We can't do—"

He slowed their actions down and began to kiss her tenderly. He kissed her long. He kissed her deeply, partly from lust, mainly from love, his tongue sweeping the inside of her mouth. His hand gripped the back of her thigh sliding it from there to her ass cheek over her soft, satiny skin still moist from her workout.

"Kade. Listen to me. We can't do th—"

"Shh!" He abruptly shushed her, his hands on her ass again, squeezing it, kneading it. "Blame this on me, Domenica. Place the blame on me if you have to feel right about it. But this is happening," he stated emphatically. Gazing into her hooded eyes, he paused to feel her. "I bet you're wet for me," he suddenly whispered into her ear, his demeanor changing. "For. Me. Domenica."

He kissed her roughly until they both gasped for breath. His other hand slid under her pants and his fingers dragged along her slit into the wetness pooling between her spread legs. He beamed a lascivious smile, staring into her eyes, as he whispered again over her lips, "See, I told you. Soaked. For. Me. I'm gonna make you come so hard, baby. Then, I'm gonna fuck you so deep."

He pulled back again studying her guilt-ridden face. Adamantly, he commanded, "Stop trying to do what others think is right. Do what *you* want. Do what *you* feel is right. Remember? *Ti amo*?" His lips moved close to her ear, licking and nibbling, as he huskily groaned, "*Ti amo*, Domenica. I. Love. You. Please love me too. Pick me, Domenica, pick me, and I will give you the world."

He cupped her breast with one hand while kissing her down her jaw line. He pulled his head back for a moment staring into her eyes as he posed his question inquisitively, "Do you truly believe it is so wrong for two people who love each other to express it?"

She slowly, slowly tilted her head and advanced into him initiating the kiss, her tongue answering his question while desperately taking over his.

This was Kade. The one who was there for her, the one who pulled her out of her darkness, the one who loved her for who she was, who didn't try to control or command—well maybe not until now. "No. I don't believe it is wrong to express love for someone. *Ti amo*, Kade."

She suddenly remembered what her mother had told her. *Never regret whatever it is that carries happiness with it into your life.* She realized that Kade was her *whatever.*

"Domenica!" He pressed his lips to hers as he promptly carried her back to her bedroom and gently laid her down on the bed, never once breaking their passionate kiss. "I need to see you."

With her help, he lifted her sports bra over her head throwing it to the floor. Next, he grabbed her boy-shorts and dragged them down and off, adding to the pile he was creating. Within a millisecond, he shed his sweats throwing them in the same direction.

She laid back leaning on her elbows as he stared at her breasts. Slowly, he scanned down the rest of her, from her flat, muscular stomach to her defined legs. "You are fucking perfect. Spread your legs open more for me, baby," he commanded staring at her sex. This was Kade, the alpha male taking over. "Fuck. You've got me so high, Domenica. So fucking high."

"Kade, stop staring. You're making me self-conscious."

"Never be afraid to display perfection, Domenica." Like a lion, Kade aggressively climbed over her, lowering his body onto hers. Then, he cradled her face as he kissed her lips, eyes, and nose. He embarked on the downward journey to end between her legs, first starting along her neck and kissing further down to her breasts. He latched on to her nipple sucking hard.

"Kade! Fuck!" Domenica threw her head back arching her back as he continued his assault on her breasts.

"Fuck is right. I'm gonna fuck you soooo good, baby." With pure lust in his eyes, he kissed down her chest to her belly button, his wet, warm tongue circling it softly, pushing it in and out, mimicking what he would do to her wet channel later with his engorged dick. "Christ, Domenica! I have never wanted anything as much as I've wanted this. As much as I've wanted you."

He slid down to position himself at her slit, sucking it into his mouth. From his attack on her whole slit, he wasted no time zeroing in on his oral assault of her clit, ravishing it like a man possessed. Once more, he used his lips and tongue on her completely engorged area, burying his face in between her stretched-out legs, smelling her scent.

"Kade!" she gasped in a hoarse groan.

He looked up at her and smiled deviously as her back arched off the bed again, her eyes lost in lust. He continued his battle on her clit.

Her hips lifted into his face as she cried out, "God... Jesus, Kade," releasing a breath she did not even know she was suppressing as she pulled at the sheets beneath her.

She tried to pull away, but he tightened his arms around her lower torso as he sucked and tongued her. He speared his tongue into her vagina and drove it in and out, knowing this was where his dick would soon be.

Kade controlled every movement in their lovemaking, a position he loved. He went back to her clit knowing she was near. "God, you are so fucking wet." He loved feeling her squirm; he loved hearing her moans—all caused by him.

"Fuck! I'm going to come!" Domenica's hips started to undulate under him. "Kade!" she screamed out as she convulsed, her body taking over her mind. Kade continued his invasion on her, all through her climax, until she aggressively pushed away crying out, "Stop! Stop! Kade, please stop!"

As her climax subsided, he gently kissed up the inside of her thigh feeling her muscles shiver involuntarily and then climbed over her again showering her lips and face with gentle pecks. She could actually taste herself still on his lips.

"I fucking love you so much. I don't even know if those are the right words, if there's any right word in any language, cuz I more than love you." Kade kissed down her neck as he whispered this. "I want in you so bad, Domenica, but I want you to want this too." He showered her with kisses again before he continued. "I want you to want *me*. Just me. Tell me you want me inside you. That you're only thinking of me."

Salaciously smiling at him, she repeated his words verbatim, "Kade Abraham, I have never wanted anything as much as I've wanted this. As much as I've wanted you, Kade."

He returned her smile answering her, "Okay then, cuz once I push my dick into you, no fucking thing on earth will be able to make me pull it out to stop until I shoot my cum inside your hot little hole." He paused and kissed her lips. "I'm gonna fuck you soooo good, baby."

With that remark, he thrust into her. "Jesus! Domenica, I am suddenly in. Fucking. Heaven." He stated the last three words with each thrust. He pressed his forehead into hers as he tried to control himself, slowly moving in and out of her while trying to regulate his gasps of breath. He wanted to feel every sensation of their coupling. "Un. Fucking. Believable!" Again said to each thrust. He wanted this to last forever, but it had been a while since his last time, and he hadn't really expected this encounter to happen today—if ever.

He growled as he pushed back in and out repeatedly. "Baby, I can feel your warm, wet walls clutching onto my dick." He slid his hand down between their bodies to play with her clit some more. "I still am remembering my tongue right *there,* baby." He pushed on her clit as he said the word *there.* "Damn, I want you. I want to stay inside of you for eternity."

Domenica was lost in his sensual words, which turned her on as much as his finger swirling around her clit. "Fuck me harder, Kade. Don't be gentle. I need you. Fuck me, Kade. I won't break." Her gasping was as uncontrolled as his was.

"Oh, I'm gonna fuck that sweet pussy hard alright. Hold on for the ride, baby." Kade stared into her eyes, not wanting to miss any of her expressions. "You are so tight, babe. So fucking wet for me."

"Kade!" she screamed out as he brought her to another orgasm, her muscles tightening around his dick clamping onto it like a vise.

"It feels amazing as fuck. God!"

Without warning, his body took over as his thrusts became faster, harder. "Fuck it, I'm there too." Overtaking him, the orgasm quickly tore into him even though he tried to slow it down. Unsuccessfully trying to maintain her gaze, his face contorted turbulently along with his body as ecstasy enveloped him. He uttered guttural groans like a trapped, feral animal, until he ultimately screamed out, "Fuuuuck!" Kade had just experienced a roaring climax, a tidal wave. No, a supernatural event so fierce that it just might have moved the earth, the moon, and every star in the universe.

As the two of them were sharing their moment, a volcano could have spewed millions of tons of ash into the stratosphere causing darkness to reign; aliens could have attacked killing every living thing in their path; a meteor could have struck the earth obliterating it. Hell, fifty hired assassins could have broken into the room and started shooting. But right now, he and Domenica had become one for the first time—had made love. All they acknowledged in the afterglow was only *this* monumental event and each other. Nothing else was important. Nothing else existed. Just the force of two becoming one.

Domenica looked up at him wiping the glistening sweat from his brow. She gently brushed her lips against his and whispered in his ear, "That good, huh?"

"*That* fucking good," he replied placing his forehead on hers. He scooped her into a bear hug and squeezed her as he grunted, rolling them both over, him on his back, her on top. "Mmmm!"

When he finally released his hug, they laid for a while, her cheek on his chest, still connected, until he softened inside her. He tenderly kissed her lips as she rolled off to lie by his side.

Grasping her hand, Kade lay there in reverie until he finally spoke, "I've fantasized about this so many times, I actually thought that if we ever did this, it would not meet up to my expectations, you know, compared to the perfect images I created of you and me in my mind. But now, we're going to have to do this again, you know, so I'm sure that the reality was better."

She smiled. "Oh, we definitely want you to be certain."

"Yeah?" he asked. He rolled to his side and slowly mounted back on top of her and started his onslaught of kisses to her face, her lips, and her neck.

Chapter 34

As Domenica swiped across the fog on the bathroom mirror, she could see Kade's sexy ass through the glass enclosure of the shower. A devilish smile spread across her face as she reviewed each moment of the last couple of hours of lovemaking with Kade, from bed to wall to shower. He definitely was all man, even though he winced every now and then from small jolts of pain from his wound. Christ, not even a gunshot wound stops a man from his sex!

These last few days, she had watched his improvement as he had been doing more activity to keep his physical stamina from slipping. She knew he had to stay in the best possible shape, just in case anyone would try to kill him. He had to be ready. From their sexual tryst, she believed he would be able to defend himself just fine.

After drying, she threw on some clothes. "Kade, I'm going out. The girls will be home in a while."

He leaned out of the shower, his wet hand grabbing her from behind her head pulling her to him to give her a passionate kiss. As he let go of her, he said, "Okay, baby. Always remember I love you." After that comment, he turned back into the shower and actually started singing. Throwing a towel around her wet head, Domenica chuckled as she closed the door after her and walked out to the living area.

What was she going to do now? She was in love with two men. Two totally different men. Matt was responsible, quiet, gentle, full of promise, like the summer's sun in clear blue skies. She needed his warm love for her to feel a sense of stability.

On the other hand, Kade was the dark shadowy clouds of winter: tumultuous, mysterious, dangerous, indiscriminately hitting her with his sense of power and adventure. She needed his exhilarating love to feel alive.

When she was with Matt, she felt tranquility, a soothing cover warming her from the harshness of life. When she was with Kade, she expected at any moment to experience the seismic movement of the earth, even when she was just lying with him in a stupid storage closet.

As she threw the towel into the laundry room, she realized one thing for sure: she should not have had sex with Kade. Now, he probably thought they would be a couple, that she chose him over Matt. In truth, she'd just made her life more difficult. One of them was going to get hurt from her decision. That was the one thing she'd wanted to avoid.

The shower stopped, the singing stopped. She heard him getting dressed. She also heard Shannon outside the door. As she opened the door, she started in on Shannon. "I hope you remembered to get the roast and potatoes from the grocery store so I can make a—"

A man, with a gun pointed at her face stood there. "Don't make a fucking sound," he answered her as he grabbed her and entered. "No roast here, little lady."

"Who are you?" Domenica demanded yelling as loud as she could, trying to warn Kade. "Listen, my roommates and I don't have money. We're poor college kids."

"I'm not here for money, cunt. If you move, I'll kill you." He started a protective sweep from room to room dragging her along. After he checked the main rooms, he pushed her aside.

Domenica edged her way to the bathroom door. Luckily, she had put the armoire back in place so they had walking room. Kade's door was open behind it, behind it where the gun was. "I'm telling you we don't have anything of value."

"Shut the fuck up," he yelled in her face.

She knew Kade had to have heard that. The bathroom area was eerily quiet. The intruder finished sweeping the apartment and turned to the bathroom with the door shut. "What's in there?" he asked her.

"The bathroom. We keep the door closed to keep it warmer than the rest of the place. You know how girls are, always cold. What are you looking for?"

He made his way to the side of the closed door as Kade pushed his body into the shower corner positioning himself so that the vanity mirror opposite the shower could not reflected his image. All he had to do now was to wait until the man came into the bathroom.

"Don't play dumb pretty lady. I know you know Kade Abraham. You hiding him here?"

"Big Kade? In here? Not luxurious enough for him I'm afraid."

He waved his gun at her, directing her to where she actually wanted to be. "Move over there by that armoire. Now! One fast movement and I *will* kill you."

Domenica slid over to the armoire, right where she could easily push it over to retrieve the loaded gun. "He's not here. I haven't seen him in at least four weeks."

"I don't fucking believe you. Kade would never pass up *your* pussy."

Kade felt his fists clenching tight. If he were out there now, the man would be dead for threatening her and talking to her like that. He would fucking put him down. Then Kade heard it.

Click, click. The doorknob started to turn.

Click, click, click. The rotation was at its end. Now just a few seconds more.

Crash! The assailant bulldozed the door in, ramming the vanity. He charged in—gun up and ready. Kade shot out of the shower pushing down on the assassin's arm as he grabbed for the gun. Now, it was only a matter of who was stronger.

While grappling for possession of the gun, they bounced into the vanity. Trying to break his hold on the gun, Kade struck both of their gun-holding hands into the shower door shattering the glass. He backed off the man and punched him in his face with the man blocking his punch, as Kade used that arm to pull the assailant into him. They both lost balance and fell over the toilet. Wedged between the toilet and vanity, neither relinquished his hold on the loaded gun. Kade was more on top, but his injury was definitely making him lose his control as the man pressed against his bad arm.

The assailant punched at Kade. As they grappled, the assailant was overpowering Kade trying to control his gun hand. The man maneuvered away from Kade and quickly stood, pushing himself off Kade, freeing the gun, and aiming for the kill shot.

Kade was going to die.

Bang! Bang! Two bullets sounded. They came through the assailant blowing out the front of his face with blood splattering everywhere.

A look of shock froze on Kade's face as the man crumbled. Ankles folded down first, coinciding with knees buckling. Hips slouched back as the man's body leaned to the right plowing into the vanity. The dead body curled into itself and slumped to the floor.

Silence.

Kade looked up to see Domenica standing just outside the door, gun in hand, still aiming into the bathroom. She was staring at the dead body, minus a face, on the floor.

Kade shot up to go to her. He slowly placed his hand on the gun. "Domenica. Let go of the gun. I got it." She did not hear as she stared at the body. "Domenica, honey, give me the gun." He steered it away from him and toward the opposite wall, finally pulling it from her hand.

"I killed him," She said matter-of-factly, still staring. "I killed someone."

At that moment, Matt burst through the front door as Kade pushed Domenica to the side and aimed the gun at the sound.

Matt, with his gun drawn, viewed the area. "Are we all clear?"

"Yeah," Kade responded. "All clear."

"Domenica!" He rushed to her, turned her around, and clutched her to his body. Then he pushed her back to look at her. "Are you hurt? Did you get hit anywhere?"

"She's okay," Kade responded. "She saved my life. You saved my life, Domenica."

In a state of shock, her knees buckled as she fell into Matt's arms. "I killed someone, Matt."

"Domenica, you saved Kade's life—and your own." He held tightly to her knowing all too well he could have lost her.

Once again, Kade viewed the scene of him being the odd man out and Domenica clutching on to Matt. He said nothing. He went into his room, grabbed his phone, and made the call. "Yeah, it's Abraham. I need a clean up here at 3417 Ruby Street, Apartment 217."

When he came back out, he saw that Matt dragged her to the couch and made her sit down with Matt alongside her.

Kade addressed Domenica. "I need the girls' phone numbers," he told her as he grabbed for her phone. He dialed Shannon first. "Yeah, it's Kade. Listen, don't come home for about two hours."

"Why? Do you have another surprise for all of us?" Shannon could not hide the excitement in her voice.

"I said don't come home!" Irritated, this time he yelled. "In fact, wait for me to call you."

"Okay! Geez! You don't have to scream at me." Shannon angrily hung up.

Then, he found Nikki and pressed the call button. "Nik? It's Kade. You need to stay away for about two hours."

"So you two are finally going to do the nasty. You go, Kade! You sure a few hours is enough time?" Nikki joked.

"Not everything is about sex, Nikki!" He yelled into the phone at her too. "Wait for me to call you."

Nikki suddenly realized that something was wrong. "Everybody okay?"

"Yes, everyone is okay here. Just stay with Dante a while. Okay? Bye." He put the phone on the table. "Matt, you wanna take her somewhere out of here?"

"Sure. You got this?"

Yeah, I got it." Kade sat on the couch as they rose and walked out the door, Matt leading Domenica. She looked like a frightened little bunny.

"We'll be at Jamal's" Matt told him as they left.

"Okay. Don't tell *anyone* what happened here."

***

Kade was somber. It was over. No more contracts out on anyone, no more killing. This was the last one. No one would know anything about him, Matt, or Domenica now. They were all safe.

So why wasn't he relieved, happy?

Because in her time of need, she swayed toward Matt again. Not to him. Nothing changed. Not after his attentiveness, his showering of gifts, his passionate lovemaking.

Nothing changed. *You can't make someone love you if it's not there,* he thought.

He sat on the couch to wait for the cleaners. He started to think about his relationship with Domenica, to evaluate the situation. In their relationship, he had always walked a fine line when it came to loving her. That had to stop, because he just realized that she belonged to the closest thing he had to a best friend, Matt. She. Loved. His. Best. Friend.

In his interactions with her, if he had come on too strong with emotion, she avoided him. If he hadn't shown her some signs of affection, she thought he was being mean, not caring enough, or angry with her. Yes, he had become proficient walking that fine line as a tightrope walker, balancing his emotions toward her so he wouldn't lose her. It had to stop. Now.

And then, to top all of this shit off, he had to go and make love to her.

He should have never fucked her, because now she was embedded deeper into his soul. "Son of a bitch!" he shouted out to no one in the room. Now, there would be another vivid memory imprinted on his fucking brain, another image to see and feel again and again.

Oh, it would eventually fade. His imagination would desperately cling to bits and pieces of her memory forever, even add on to his reality with fantasy. It would be like it was before. When he kept his distance, his memory of her conspired with his dreams to prevent him from forgetting her. Only so that when he was awake, he would think of nothing but her. The Domenica memory hiding in his brain just wanted to fuck him up his ass once again. "Fuck!" he shouted again.

He picked up the light from the side table and threw it against the dance area mirror shattering it to pieces. "I fucking hate her!" He slouched back on the couch, his hands pressed against his head.

"No, I don't hate her. I could never hate her. Ever."

Chapter 35

I came to say goodbye." Kade hugged Domenica tight knowing it would be the last time he would ever touch her. She did not see his face as he squeezed his eyes shut so his other senses could soak in the feel of her body, the smell of her hair, the taste of her skin, when he planted a kiss on her cheek.

He released her slowly, his hands now holding hers.

"You don't have to go, Kade."

"Yes I do. You know I do. You know *why* I have to go." His stare pierced her heart.

Domenica's cheeks burned red as she quickly glanced around to see where Matt was, if he heard. "I'm just saying I will miss you more than you will ever know."

"Matt's in the other room, and this is what I mean. Us watching what we say and do. You can't play it both ways. It's not in your personality to do that. Look. I know you're trying not to hurt anybody's feelings, but in this case, somebody has to get hurt. Me. You had to make a choice, and it was Matt."

"But I didn't make the—"

"Yes. Yes you did. Unconsciously you did." He stood studying her every move to forge into his memory. "You know, Domenica, it's amazing to me that your eyes have all the right working parts, all in the right places, both eyes apparently hooked up to the optic nerve, and yet you can't see what is right in front of your fucking nose!" His voice was abrupt.

She glanced down not knowing what to say.

"Listen, I might come back to visit. A few years from now. Maybe next year. I'm going to be at my New York office. It's one of the busy ones, so I'll have plenty to do." He hugged her again. "You take care of Lima Bean for me. Near death experiences seem to follow him around like a lost dog. The next one might just be a death experience! I can't take care of him anymore, so you are going to have to."

With tears in her eyes, she pulled Kade into her again. "You take care of yourself. I *do* love you, Kade. At least know that," she said letting go of him.

Maybe more than I should, she thought.

She turned abruptly. "I'm sorry, but I can't watch you walk away. I'm going to say goodbye now." She held on to his hand for a long time as tears fell down her cheeks. She couldn't even kiss him good-bye the way she wanted to, for fear that Matt might see. She released him and turned to go into her bedroom.

"*Ti amo*, Domenica," he softly called after her as she walked away. "Forever."

Matt came out of the kitchen and grasped Kade's hand. He pulled him in for a bear hug as Domenica slipped into her room. "Hey, my friend, thanks again for saving not only my life, but for helping to protect the woman I love."

"Any time, Lima Bean, any time." He affectionately slapped him on his back.

Matt quickly looked around to see if Domenica was in her room as he moved closer to Kade. "Listen, Kade, I'm going to ask Domenica to marry me, and depending on her answer, well, I wanted you to be my best man. I'm asking you in advance so you can schedule it." He smiled at Kade.

"Sure. Sure, Matt. Just let me know when and where. I'll be there."

"Okay then. Listen, keep in touch with us. You are more of a family to me than my own family. I love you, Kade."

"Love you too, brother." Kade hugged him, slipped out of the door, and headed down to his car. This time Kade faced her like a man should. He didn't sneak away, although it didn't make him feel any better.

He sat in his car thinking about Domenica. He would leave forever. After all, he loved the same woman his friend loved, would always love her.

Would he find another love like that? He didn't know. He did know this: he could never replace a perfect diamond with a lump of coal that, in time, might eventually turn into a diamond.

As for being the best man, he said yes, but he would never be able to do that. Watch her marry someone else. On the date of their wedding, he would make up some excuse about being out of the country on important business or something.

Domenica always talked about how she was majoring in life. Well, he learned an important life lesson with all of this shit. Love doesn't end happily for the majority of people. Because love and romance were the biggest con artists life had to offer. Love never told anyone that it might only lasted a while or, as in his case, that it might be one-sided. Love and romance just conned people into believing that there was always hope. There wasn't.

Either way, it was never forever. And even if these love stories did tell us that love never lasted, no one would believe or accept it.

Lovers all believe *theirs* was the one that would make it. Christ! If he saw true love on the Titanic, he would still board it to seize that true love, knowing very well that the ship was doomed to hit an iceberg and sink. He would be the first in line to walk up that gangplank—on a doomed ship—if it meant a chance with Domenica.

He started the car thinking about how he hated the harsh New York winters. Although enduring those winters was a much better fate than watching her live with and love another man. That he could never endure.

***

From her bedroom window, Domenica watched him slide into the car, back out of the driveway, and drive off. A déjà vu moment for sure, like when Matt had to leave on the bus that first time. She turned away from the window back into the room. As she leaned against the adjacent wall, her face lifted with her eyes traveling up to the solid white color of the ceiling. She whispered in a faint tone, "What if I chose wrong?"

THE END

Make sure you read *Lessons Applied, Book 3*, the last of the *Majoring in Life* series. Who does she choose? Matt or Kade?

*C*an you do me a favor and leave a review?

Just one positive review on Amazon is like buying the book 100 times! Reader support is so important to beginning authors. And remember, I think and write outside the box because I love challenging my creative side. A positive review for this new author would mean everything to me. Go to the sales page of this book on Amazon and *scroll down until you see* "Review this Product" – "Leave a Customer Review."

*T*hanks!

~~~~~~

*O*ther Works by the Author

Majoring in Life Series
Lessons Taught
Lessons Learned
Lessons Applied

~~~~~~

Contact Information:
https://www.amazon.com/~/e/B07XF67PRX
https://www.facebook.com/e.marrocchella
emarrocchella@hotmail.com
www.emarrocchella.com

ABOUT THE AUTHOR

I am proud to be a second generation Italian-American. My four grandparents came over from Sicily, Naples, Calabria, and Foggia. They all learned the English language and American history. They studied to become American citizens. They raised my parents in Italian tradition, and my parents raised my siblings and me the same way. God, family, education, respect, and the arts were taught and demonstrated in our Italian home. It is where I learned to love reading stories.

Although I started to read at an early age, I started writing when I was fifteen years old. Perhaps writing just became associated with reading passion. My love of reading and writing drove me to become an English teacher. I married, raised children, and had to put reading and writing away for a long time, because my children came first. In fact, life always came first over hobbies.

Now, I have time to write and read. My husband bought me a Kindle and with that one gift, my passion heated up again. This first writing project is based on the stories my daughter and former students told me about college life. College classes taught nothing as compared to being thrown into an environment where one had to coexist with people of all ages and from all walks of life. Learning about life at college became a major for everyone! One we didn't get credit for.